A Mafia Hand: JUNO

High Stakes Series

Book One

Shilo West

Crave Publishing

A MAFIA HAND: Juno

First Print Edition: January 2023

Crave Publishing

Kailua, HI 96734

www.cravepublishing.net

ISBN-13: 978-1-64034-647-5

This is a work of fiction. Names, characters, places, and incidents either are the product of the author's imagination or are used fictitiously, and any resemblance to locales, events, business establishments, or actual persons—living or dead—is entirely coincidental.

ONE

She's been dealt hundreds of hands in the Rodeo Room of the Wagon Wheel Casino, but tonight, when it counted the most, those sweet poker-playing cowboy ghosts kept sending her face cards, high threes and fours, straights and flushes. If she had been any one of her opponents around the tournament table, she would have suspected some kind of cheating. But these boys had resigned themselves to getting a good thrashing from a beautiful woman. Tonight, she had prayed her lucky red pumps had just enough traction left, both in their magic and in their heels, to take her through one last big jackpot. Juno Cooper had never needed a win this badly before, not even in her early days on the circuit.

The first round of bets in, the dealer turned four cards. The burn card went face down on the table, then dealt the flop. One of the three face-up cards on the board put Juno close to a straight flush. She had the seven and nine of spades; the eight lay on the table between a king and an ace. As long as the next two cards came up either the five or ten of spades, she'd have a killer hand, almost unbeatable. It was her turn to bet, and she kept cool, calling. The player to her left folded, but the last player raised, and by enough to cause a little head shaking around the table. *Fine*, she thought, *you can just hand me your wallet*. She tried not to look at him again. Situated at about ten o'clock from her, he'd been a thorn in her side all night. He was pretty enough to look at, but Juno wasn't in the mood for nonsense, and this guy couldn't help himself. She was having to spend way too much of her focus just keeping her thoughts from wandering back to the dimple in his chin.

Despite her efforts, the flush was showing in more than the cards she held; she could feel the crimson rising up her neck as the shaggy boy across the table shifted slowly in his club chair. His hips moved slightly to music coming from the casino floor, but his eyes stayed on Juno. She wasn't looking at him, but after years in casinos, country clubs, dive bars, and back room card games up and down the East Coast before making her way here to Vegas, Juno had learned a thing or two, or four or five, about how to keep track of all the eyes at a card table. "Don't ever meet their eyes." She could hear her mother's voice clearly right now, coaching her while she practiced no-look Faro shuffles in front of a mirror when she was no more than nine or ten. "Don't look at the cards. And, whatever you do, don't look at the other players." Juno's hazel eyes, sharp as desert mica, were a weapon she used sometimes, a way to distract any man she opposed. But tonight, she hid them behind cheap Jackie O knockoffs, big black ovals covering most of her face. A trick she'd use when she needed to be left in her private thoughts. And this tournament had no room for distractions. This tournament was her prison break. Her ticket out of a life she never meant to have.

The dealer showed the turn, setting it alongside the other cards. Juno's heart jumped at first—a black ten, but clubs. No matter. She wasn't superstitious. There was one more card to go. But first, the round of bets. The big blind called, but the small blind, the second player from the dealer, raised the 140k bet to 200k. He'd been struggling all night; Juno would have felt sorry to see him slide his chips forward with so much confidence if her heart hadn't shrunken into a raisin. And whatever winner he thought he had would not be enough. *He's got kings*, she thought. *A pair of kings. He's hoping the river card is another one. But it won't be. It's a ten of spades*, Juno thought, *because it's my card.*

Nobody knows why the last round in Texas Hold 'Em is called the "river." Juno's mother told her it came from the riverboat days; that's where they they'd throw you if you cheated. Juno's mother said if you were smart, there was no need to cheat. Cheaters were stupid, but the worst people in the world were people who got caught. They were not only stupid, but careless.

"What's the matter, gorgeous? Thinking about where you're going to take me to dinner? I'm looking at being broke and hungry later. Put me out of my misery, please." Kansas Bill's voice almost startled Juno. She'd been playing in tournaments with Bill for years, and he must have noticed something was off about her. She recovered with a slow smile, but there was that laugh again. She tried to sneak a look at this new guy once again from behind her dark glasses. And he was every inch worth the effort: golden skin, perfectly manicured dark hair short on the sides, longer on top, a carefully trimmed beard, and brown eyes deep as caverns. Probably one of these band boys, or a rich kid —he had the ease of somebody with too much money to feel any pressure. Italian tailored suits like that one didn't come cheap. Not to mention the beautiful Rolex watch. And that little dance he kept doing, singing along with the music that filtered in from the casino floor. The Killers. Hometown boys who were back in town tonight playing the stadium, and the whole city was celebrating. She remembered the days when they were still playing bars, hungry to make it. She liked them because of that, because she knew they had to work hard to make it, just like she did. Nobody there to hand it to them. It didn't hurt that they were pretty. But you had to be more than pretty. She had learned.

The dealer stretched his neck from side to side. His hand was on the card. Juno shut her eyes and waited for the sound of the flick, along with the slight exhales around the table as no one saw what they hoped for. Because it was Juno's card. The ten of spades sat there on the table, right where she needed it to be.

She didn't smile. She barely regarded the card, or anyone else. She listened disinterestedly to the bets around the table. The big blind folded. The small blind raised again. *Those three kings are not bringing Christmas early for you, honey*, Juno thought to herself. She'd been focusing on a Blackjack dealer just outside the Rodeo room, the first table on the casino floor. Her point in the middle distance, just like her mother taught her. He'd deal, then sweep the cards back into the shoe, over and over. There were only two people at his table, a hunched man in a polo and a woman with a large, feathered bag. They moved only their hands, hit or stand, around and around like a cuckoo clock. Steady as rocks.

"Fold. Madame, I like steak. I'll make us a reservation if you like." Juno smiled a little but didn't look at Bill. She considered her next move carefully. Going all-in would be too obvious. Even a big raise would be, at this point. She just needed that pretty boy to call, and this hand alone would raise her lifestyle standards for the next few years. And she'd be well situated for the grand prize money. She unlocked her jaw slowly before speaking. "I see two hundred. Raise to two-fifty." Her chips clacked against her nails as she placed them in front of her. The next player had folded in the last round, so the final bet came to the golden boy. He stared fixedly at Juno, turning his bourbon glass like he was winding a watch. He used a chip to ask for more time.

"Boy's got the nuts," the big blind player said.

"Naw," said Bill, "he's taking too long. He's got what they call a Mafia hand. It's too late; he can't get out now."

Juno looked up as he broke into a genuine cackle of glee. A smile of childlike wonder spread across his tanned face, and his big, deep-set eyes wrinkled. For a minute, Juno let her mind wander. If only she'd met him at a party or on the plane after this was all over. The timing couldn't have been worse.

"I fold," he said, still laughing and shaking a finger at Bill. "Now, now. It's never too late to change, you know."

Damn it, she thought. *That's what I get for counting the chips before the bets are in. Well, there's always the next hand.* And if he went all in, he'd have lost, and she'd have nothing to look at. She'd never see him again. Right now, she avoided looking at the small blind when her turn came to reveal her cards.

Whistles around the table gave way to praise for Juno's hand. "Straight flush: damn, woman," "She had a secret," and then, "Daaaamn, I *knew* you were sitting on something special over there," from the man in leather. Finally, Juno looked at him.

"Sweetheart, you have no idea." The players

whooped in unison, and Juno turned back to watch the Blackjack dealer and his table. She just had to think about something else. But that sexy laugh crawled under her skin, traveling down her spine, all the way down to her slender feet in her slightly worn-out shoes.

Two

"Gentlemen, a straddle is in play," the dealer intoned, gesturing around the table before dealing.

"Hot damn! Words I have been waiting to hear all night long," her nemesis cackled. Oh, that laugh. Juno pressed her knees together under the table.

"Why don't you just sit there looking hot, and the adults will play the game?"

"Darling, you wound me. And here I thought we were getting to be friends."

"No friends at the table, pretty boy."

She knew better than to keep talking to him, and yet she itched to have the last word. He'd drawn her into banter, the worst trick; he was gaming her. *Not today, you caramel sundae of a man*, she thought. *I could have eaten you with a spoon, once upon a time, but tonight I'm on a steady diet of chips. And when I'm full, I'm cashing out of this circus. No attachments. I'm walking out of here into a new life. The world is full of spoiled rich boys, even if you are one of the yummiest I've ever seen.*

Juno had little patience for his type. Never worked for anything, never felt a moment's strain, no callouses on those delicious, long fingers. *Stop it, Juno,* she told herself. Before she could help it, she found herself thinking back to the first time she saw Mitchell. She'd thought the same thing about him, only to find out quickly that she had been wrong. She'd met Mitchell Byron in a baccarat room in Monte Carlo. Not a place poor boys from Plano or orphans from Tennessee end up in, nearly ever. To her, Mitchell had seemed too confident, as if he was exactly where he belonged. Even in her recently acquired Tom Ford couture slip dress, Juno remembered how she was shaking inside before her first Monte Carlo tournament. Moving among the billionaires and heads of state, Juno felt like an imposter, a fraud. She was only there to play a game.

"Taste this and tell me what you think." Those were Mitchell's first words to her, spoken during a dealer change. They came with a fluted glass, pinkish-golden with bubbles. Juno threw her head back.

"I never drink when I'm playing," she replied, staying him with her hand. His hand enfolded hers, warm and soft. He smiled, even warmer and softer.

"I see. Please accept my apologies. My name is Mitchell. Mitchell Byron."

In the moment, the name rang in her memory. It was only later, after the baccarat game concluded, that she learned from Samantha, the room's private bartender, why.

"Juno, the guy trying to talk to you? That's XK3."

"No. I thought nobody knew his identity?"

"Well, that's him. That's all I know. He's been in town for months. Nobody knows why, but they think he's meeting with some people from Qatar about a land deal or something. He's building some kind of facility there, I don't know. Oh, I do know one more thing. That the man has some..." Samantha smiled at Juno and looked away. "Some specific tastes, if you know what I mean."

When Juno returned to her room that night, there was a single, fresh glass of champagne set on a marble table. In a silver bucket, the entire bottle sat on ice. "Dom Perignon, Rose Gold Methuselah, 1996," Juno mumbled to herself, reading the label. "I don't think I even have to Google that to know how expensive..."

"Oh, it's upwards of $60,000 a bottle in the dining room. But we're not in the dining room."

She'd managed that night not to show how afraid she was to find a strange, beautiful man in her room. She internalized the fear, letting it intoxicate her along with that bottle of champagne that could have sent two kids to college. She barely paused before letting the Tom Ford slip dress fall from her shoulders like froth into a glass.

She'd been wrong about Mitchell. She'd been so wrong about everything, but the first mistake she had made was underestimating his work ethic. Mitchell

Byron, known to the world as the mysterious inventor, entrepreneur, and tech billionaire XK3, had come, it turned out, from nothing and nowhere. His father died weeks before his pension from Texas Technologies would have kicked in. Mitchell had gone to community college while taking care of his ailing mother. Not all of the time was accounted for, but at some point in the year after her death was reported, Mitchell Byron left Plano, and no one knew where he had gone. That was, until he turned up years later, having legally changed his name to XK3 before his precipitous rise to wealth and fame.

Not many people knew XK3 was a boy from Plano. Not many people knew how he'd had to scrape and scramble to build his empire. And it was an empire. And he was a king. With a court full of attendants and villagers. And soldiers. Who were hunting for Juno right now. Because Juno knew. She knew all of it.

THREE

Juno stared back at herself from the bathroom mirror. She splashed a little more water on her face, careful to avoid her eyelashes. She'd folded early to give herself a moment to recover her composure, and she had to make herself ready to go back and finish this thing.

"Girl, come on," she whispered, smacking her face lightly until her cheeks were a little red. "He's got you all flustered, and today is not the day. You've seen nicer butts. Well, maybe not, actually, but there will be plenty of them—and some almost just as nice—when you get safely to Costa Rica." She was talking a little louder than a whisper now, and as a young woman came out of the last stall, she caught her eye in the mirror. "Move along, honey. Nothing to see here. Oh, and by the way, you be careful with that old man you're hanging on at the craps table. He's married, and the money's hers. And she's mean as a snake." The girl sniffled at Juno and snapped her purse closed before heading for the door.

When it was quiet again, Juno looked back at her reflection. "Now, that money on the table belongs to you," she told herself. She heard the words in her mother's gravelly purr; she could almost hear the lighter flicking and the hiss as the cigarette lit. "You go get your money, Juno. Don't let Mama down."

Cold casino air conditioning braced Juno as she swanned out of the lounge and turned toward the Rodeo Room. Where she stopped dead in her tracks. Mitchell's men. They looked almost exactly like casino security except for their shoes, but she recognized them immediately. Instead of going straight up the aisle, she turned as casually as she could down a long row of slot machines, doing her best not to draw any attention to herself. Lights flashed from every direction as the machines played circus music, horn fanfares, Elvis songs, and sweeping harp runs. Which didn't help her pounding heart. Sounds of spaceships, chickens, screams—she never understood slot machines. Complete chaos. No sport, no strategy, no psychology. Just flash and noise.

She sat down in front of an Egyptian-themed machine, setting her leather sack slightly open in front of her on the foot ledge. She pretended to study the available bets on the machine while she counted the chips below her in the bag. She'd left a lot on the table, but she could figure no way back into the Rodeo Room. *The greedy pig*, she thought.

The greedy pig gets slaughtered, her mother used to say.

"Champagne?" This time, Juno jumped and gasped out loud, not realizing she'd been holding her breath for so long trying to stifle her panic while also trying not make any noise. It was just the cocktail girl, who laughed and patted her back. "Dang, honey, I didn't mean to scare you. You just look like a gal who needs some champagne. And a tip." She leaned in, and Juno's eyes widened. "You don't want to play that machine. Lady just hit real big on it around lunch time, and it ain't paid squat since."

Juno nodded. "Thanks, hon," she said, smiling widely at the waitress. "I'll take that champagne, but bring it to me over at that Blackjack table." She pointed across to the dealer she'd been watching all night, the one just next to the Rodeo Room. When the waitress walked away, she grabbed her bag and walked slowly and confidently in the opposite direction.

———

Monk Mason Davies loved bourbon. He'd make a big show of getting some kind of expensive shot, "double, one ice cube, a medium-size one, not one of those boulders," right at the start of a round of poker so that everyone at the table would think he'd been drinking all day and night. Then he'd nurse that Pappy Van Winkle, fifteen or twenty-one year, or if they didn't have it, whatever Weller Antique or Willet Pot Still—

"No? None of those? Well, bring me Four Roses, and I'll give you one, sweetheart. Two if I win."

Monk was holding and not drinking the bourbon he'd been holding and not drinking for a good four or five hours, trying not to look at the doorway to the Rodeo Room situated behind him. He kept looking up at old Kansas Bill, knowing he'd be able to tell by the look on Bill's face if that girl was on her way back to the table. Monk remembered staying up late when he was a kid and watching Kansas Bill on the World Series of Poker. He'd fall asleep to the clinking of the chips and low laughter of men, both on his television and coming from the back room of his parents' bar, just below his bedroom. The years had worn Bill down a little, Monk thought, but he loved the man's zest for life, his old chunk of cigar always sitting on the edge of his mouth, and the way he could liven up a poker table full of dough-faced, boring, safe-betting math heads. Monk didn't care about the statistics. It's supposed to be fun; that's why it's called a "card game," not a "card job."

In fact, tonight was promising to be more fun than Monk had dreamed. He'd never played at the table with her before, but he was almost certain he's seen the mysterious woman in her dark glasses before. Her hair might have been different. No matter that he couldn't place the memory—he determined he'd be making some new ones tonight. Watching her play, he felt like he knew her already. She wasn't as showy as Bill, but she was fearless. *Nothing*, Monk thought to himself, *is sexier than a fearless woman.* He knew she was noticing him, too. She saw him moving while he was pretending to slow dance with her in his head. The little corner of her mouth would twitch a little. Everybody else at the table probably thought it was a tell that meant she was bluffing. But that tiny smirk was telling Monk something else entirely.

She was cleaning his clock; he ought to be mad at her. *The truth is,* Monk thought to himself, *I've never quite so thoroughly enjoyed a beating from a woman.* Well, maybe once or twice. He was grinning to himself with a deep inhale when he noticed it, that scent, earthy like oranges and tobacco, but electric like heat lightning. He couldn't help himself. But as he turned to smile at Juno's return, she was gone already. He thought he glimpsed her dark crown of curls disappearing into the casino crowd. *Maybe that is a wig,* he thought.

The casino floor manager and the concierge seemed to be engaged in some kind of serious discussion with a couple of bodyguard types. Monk feigned disinterest but leaned back in his chair to hear what he could above the thumping drums and bass coming through from the main gaming floor. He thought he heard "she" a few times, and a long "hmm" of uncertainty from the manager. But shortly a waiter came and cleared away everything left of Monk's most fascinating opponent of the evening: only a glass of water and several generous stacks of chips.

Something isn't right, Monk thought. *Nobody*

leaves that kind of money on the table. It's one thing to walk away when you're up, but the girl in the cheap Jackie O sunglasses and possible wig had the tournament prize money nearly locked up. He narrowed his eyes at the black-suited men, but they were busy looking around the room, under her chair, and under the table. Until they got a little too close to Kansas Bill.

"What's the matter with you boys? Did you lose an alien? Listen, son, get your hand off my leg unless you're taking me dancing later." Monk met Bill's eyes for a second and saw the same look of concern. There was no time to ask Bill anything more, and anyway, with these goons around, it wasn't possible. Monk Davies loved pretty women and a smoking-hot card table, but one of those was leaving and the other would be here just as well when he came back. And if he got really lucky, he'd find the one more thing he loved. The thing he had lost for so long and could not seem to capture again: real danger. He took out his phone and looked at it long enough to be convincing and shook his head at the guys next to him at the table. "Ah, man, I gotta take this. I'm out this hand, anyway. Keep my drink warm, would ya?" Then Monk headed out onto the crowded casino floor.

FOUR

To get to the cash-out windows, Juno had to skirt the edges of the main casino floor. The clacking roulette wheels were interrupted every few seconds with cries of joy or disaster, everybody waiting to see where the spinning would stop. Red, black, red, black. *It only seems random*, Juno thought to herself. *People think it's up to chance, how your life ends up.* She'd been called lucky all her life. The word tasted bitter in her mouth, because she knew luck was a lie. Work, that's what mattered. *You make your own luck*, she could hear her mother saying.

The casino lobby was too open; she'd need to pass through the grand marble arcade of shops and the enormous aquarium, dolphins swimming in tubes overhead. Maybe if she moved slowly between the clumps of tourists taking selfies, she could little by little access the exit without having to be exposed. She pulled a visor out of her bag, put it on, then gathered the wig into a ponytail through the back. She removed her lucky red heels and slipped on a pair of Keds sneakers. Then she took her jacket and tied it around her waist, checking her revised silhouette in the mirrored window of the Chanel store.

In the reflection, she saw three more of Mitchell's men spreading out at each set of glass doors in the lobby, and she knew she'd have to leave another way. She started weaving through a smaller room with rows of Blackjack tables and slot machine kiosks, all clanging merrily as if to mock her. She didn't run; she knew that would be the end of her. She walked with her head up, pretending to consider the gaming options. At the end of the Blackjack tables, more men in suits.

She slid into the fake leather captain's chair in front of a *Wheel of Fortune* slot machine. In the chrome, she saw more men coming up behind her, far back toward the entrance of the room. She scanned for a restroom. A door marked "Employees Only" looked promising, as long as it wasn't locked. But what if it was just a closet full of vacuum cleaners? Juno stared at Pat and Vanna, their glossy smiles peeking around the big wheel on the slot machine. "Spin the wheel," Pat was saying. "Do you feel lucky?" *I feel sick*, Juno thought to herself. *But I brought this on myself. No hard luck, no bad luck. Just bad choices.* Vanna's smile looked more sympathetic. She looked like one of those Greek deities in her white column gown, bedecked with rubies and emeralds. Or cut glass, as the case probably was. *What kind of name is Vanna?* "Help me, goddess," Juno whispered. "Send me an angel."

Juno twisted the arm into a bar hold almost before the hand touched her elbow. "Whoa! Hey! That's a kung-fu grip there, ow ow OW, can you maybe let go?" Monk tried not to scream in pain and draw attention to her, but she just about tore his arm off.

"Oh, it's *you*," Juno hissed. "Honey, today is not the day."

And what a shame, because that dimple in his chin was even more irresistible up close. "Look, I don't know exactly what kind of trouble you're in, but it so happens trouble is a hobby of mine..."

Juno shook her head and tried to edge past Monk to an adjacent slot machine, a little farther from the aisle where Mitchell's men were coming from opposite directions. "You need to go, baby doll," Juno said, tilting her head down and glancing at Monk over the edges of her sunglasses. "I mean, run away. You are beyond over your pretty head. Run on back to your trust fund, or your hedge fund, or whatever fund is dragging you along into grown-up games and other peoples' business. And you're drawing way too much attention, and you are going to *get me killed*." She whispered the last part through her teeth and punch him lightly in the chest to emphasize each word. He just kept talking over her—why did men do that?

"...and the way I see it, you could use some help. I know every inch of this casino, ma'am," Juno rolled her eyes behind her glasses as he imitated her accent, "almost as well as I know the curve of your neck after sitting across from you for six hours." Juno drew back as he put his hand on her hip. "*Play along,*" he whispered in her ear. Then he nudged her cheekbone with his, turned his head slightly, and placed his soft lips on her mouth. For a second, Juno forgot Mitchell's men. She forgot the poker tournament, the money in her bag, the cabana boys waiting in Costa Rica. She almost forgot to breathe. His arms enclosed her like a second skin, like a protective, warm, shadow, while Mitchell's arms had always hung oddly on her like a secondhand winter coat. She stood rapt, eyes closed, taking in the pressure of his lips, his chest, his hips, the smell of leather and bourbon, the ringing casino bells.

When her eyes finally opened, she saw Mitchell's men walking together, back into the main casino, tapping their ear monitors and looking each way like schoolchildren in a crosswalk. Monk, already walking away, grabbed her hand. "Come on," he said. "I've got some friends who can help. Just come with me."

What choice do I have? Juno thought. She was so tired of those words.

Monk nodded at a dealer who was making his way off the floor. "Hey, Danny, can we, uh..." Monk gestured toward the Employees Only door.

Danny smiled and waved his key fob. "Headed that way myself. What you getting into tonight, boss? Anything fun?"

Danny led Juno and Monk through the tunnels in the casino's undercroft. Juno's mind was casting in as many directions as the winding passageways, bright under the fluorescent lights. Danny swiped his fob again over the pad next to a large door marked "Alarm Will Sound," but Monk threw it open without hesitation. "Somebody really ought to fix that," he called to Danny, who saluted him from halfway down the next passage. "After you," he said to Juno, holding the door open.

When Juno stepped out into the dark alley, the real world pulled in close again. She turned to Monk. "Listen to me. I know you think this is some kind of cool adventure or something, but these men..." She looked both ways into the Vegas night, dappled with neon, streaked with spotlights crossing each other. "They won't stop. They're going to take me, or they're going to kill me. And I'm gonna tell you, they're gon have to kill me."

"No, now, you listen just a sec—"

"You get in their way and, baby, they will bash in your pretty face. That's if you're lucky. Trust me: if we'd met a few years ago, this night would be ending very, very differently. I mean to tell you." She looked him up and down one last time. He slapped his forehead in frustration; when he raised his arm, she saw the gun tucked into his waistband. She squinted at him for one more second, then dove out into the night, wondering if her timing would ever, ever be right in this life.

She didn't need to pretend anymore. Juno ran toward the brightest end of the alley. She had no idea what side of the casino she was on, but she hoped she'd come out into a busy part of Fremont Street. There, she could disappear into the Saturday night crowds, which were starting to peak. She had made it almost to the end of the three-block-long casino building when she heard a roll-up garage door moving just before she was blinded by what seemed like several flashlights coming at her. Two ATVs sped toward her. She spun around, only to see more of them coming from the far end of the alley. Juno crossed the alley to the other wall, hugging it as she groped for a door or window that might be unlocked. The vehicles would meet in a moment, and they would seize her. She turned and ran toward the ATVs. Just before she reached them, another garage door rolled up. A shiny red Porsche Spider screeched into the alley, spinning to a stop as the passenger door flung itself open in front of her. She threw herself inside, and the ATVs swarmed around them as Monk floored the vehicle, leaving Mitchell's men behind as he emerged onto Fremont. Pedestrians cheered and the crowd parted as the gleaming car skidded into a hard right turn, then accelerated toward the lights of the Strip on the horizon. Juno realized her mouth was open; she almost had to use her hand to close it.

"I don't think we've been introduced, but my name is Monk Mason Davies. I know how you Southern women are, so I figured maybe that's why you won't let me save you. Hey, did you really think throwing yourself under an ATV would kill you? I mean, you might break a bone or something, but..."

"Monk Mason Davies, somebody needs to hit you upside the head, but I'm...I'm..."

"Grateful, I know. That's the word you're looking for."

"Pretty sure that's not it, but it'll do. For now."

Monk slowed a little and merged off the highway. "Wait," she said. "I thought of the word. The word is 'hungry.'" Monk laughed, that glorious, sexy laugh. Full of mischief and secrets.

FIVE

"Let's get clear of downtown. I know a place in Chinatown. It's a hoot, and nobody will— Oh, hey, okay, I see you're getting rid of some unnecessary, uh, let me just roll that window down for you."

As soon as the car window reached halfway down, Juno started throwing out her smart watch, her SIM card that she'd already removed from her cell phone, and finally, in frustration, the entire phone itself. She emptied her entire bag into her lap and tossed out a lipstick, a couple of pens, and a compact. She took a large ring from her finger and threw it out, too. "I see," Monk repeated. "Yeah, I didn't think that one was really your style. That's right; let it all go."

Juno sat still, staring at road in front of them. Finally, she slid the wig from her head to reveal her ash blond hair stuck to her head in eyelash ringlets. She held her arm out the window, and Monk gunned the engine again as she released the wig into the wind.

At first, The Golden Tiki hadn't looked like much to Juno. But inside, the strip mall restaurant turned out to be a trendy bar. A tattooed DJ was spinning spooky surf guitar music to the crowd bathed in purple light. Monk led Juno through cave walls, past a waterfall and an enormous conch shell. After some conversation with a talking skeleton, he showed her into an even darker, quieter room with a row of shrunken heads along the ceiling.

"Shanna!" Monk called out. "I know you're back there. I'm going to my spot, and I have a... I've got a friend with me." Monk slid the corner booth table out for Juno to sit, and a woman dressed as a mermaid appeared with a menu. "Shanna," Monk greeted her with a kiss on the cheek, whispering loud enough for Juno to hear, "it's our first date; make me look important, will ya?" Mermaid Shanna smirked, then turned to Juno.

"See anything you like on the menu, hun?"

"I'll have the Captain's Balls," Juno said, decidedly, handing the menu back. "And something pretty with gin in it. And one of those little umbrellas."

"I like you!" Shanna said, giving Monk a nudge. "She's awesome. I'll fight you for her."

"Don't hurt me again, Shanna. Oh, and I'll have the Voodoo that You Do. Extra spicy." Monk smiled across the table. "Okay. This is better, isn't it?"

Juno thought if she let the crack in her icy fortress thaw any more, she'd be crying like a teenager in front of Monk. She didn't want to be saved. But if somebody had to do it, she had to admit, he wasn't a bad option. He did seem to know his way around. She was grateful but didn't trust her gratitude. But everybody had to eat. She'd stay, get some food in her, and start out before daybreak. She was weighing the options, train or bus, and not listening to anything Monk was saying.

"...so that's why I come here, even though that night was pretty crazy. Convenient, right? The cops would not even think of looking for you here."

Juno looked at Monk. Then she laughed, the hardest she'd laughed in weeks. Maybe months. Her ribs hurt a little. She was still laughing when Shanna placed a drink in front of her, something that looked like a Tastee Freeze vanilla twist covered in pink orchids coming out of a tall wooden mug with a grimacing Tiki face. Crowned with a halo of flaming marshmallows on sticks, it was so ridiculous that she laughed until she couldn't breathe. Then the tears started. But she inhaled sharply and took a long sip of her beverage, which turned out to be surprisingly delicious. "Oh, honey," she began, looking up at Monk. "If only the police were chasing me."

"Well, FBI, CIA..."

"No, no. No letters. Except B, A, and D. These guys are not any sort of law enforcement."

Monk had a look of minor consternation. "Well, they aren't from any organization doing any business in Vegas. I mean, uh, they don't seem to be. I've done a little security work around here and...yeah, these guys..."

"I'm supposed to believe that? What kind of security work buys you a car like that? You're not fooling me, mister. You must think I'm a lot younger and a lot dumber than I am." Monk sat back and was quiet for a minute. *Must have hit a nerve*, she thought. *These trust fund boys and their egos.* But Shanna was there with big, heavy platters of steaming food. The spicy smells and the satisfying thump of the plates landing on the table sent Juno into a near swoon. While she satisfied her hunger, Monk seemed to think for a minute about what to say next.

"It's a special car, yes. I'm lucky enough to know the guy who owns it. Well, not so much luck. He owes me a favor." Juno was tired of trying to decide whether or not a man was lying. After what she'd been through, she knew very well when key pieces of the puzzle were missing. She studied Monk while she wrapped her lips around the thick straw in her cocktail. He smiled—leered, ever so slightly.

"I suppose you think I owe you a favor?" she murmured.

And then he suddenly turned bashful, shaking his shaggy head as if to cast off what he was really thinking about. "Now, now. Not that I don't admire your... well, everything, but let's take a second here. You're not in any shape for... Let's just say, I'd rather your heart be in it."

Juno rolled her eyes. "Oh, baby. I'm being rescued by an emo poet. I'm sunk. I'm a dead woman."

They both laughed, until Monk leaned forward, almost touching her face across the small table. "No way," he whispered, and Juno again let herself be pulled into the soft, warm embrace of his deep brown eyes. *Kiss me, kiss me*: those were the only words in her mind as her whole body resonated with desire. She could feel the bass guitar and drums in her core, her hips sliding forward on the velvet seat, her thighs tingling as if he were already holding them. "No way," he said again, barely shaking his head and smiling. "I've found you, and I won't leave you. They will have to come through me. And I don't care who they are; that's going to be a lot harder than they have any earthly idea. I promise you that."

SIX

Speeding down the strip in a red sportscar might not seem like a good way to lay low. But Monk had a plan. Juno leaned as far back as the seat would go and watched all the bright neon cascade across the windshield.

Juno had a plan. But Monk had changed it, at least for now. He hadn't kissed her there at the table in the Golden Tiki. Well, he almost did. Just as she closed her eyes, his lips grazed her forehead. And when she looked, he was back in his chair, ravenously attacking a barbecued rib. She had wanted to crawl across the palm-patterned tablecloth and taste the sauce on his full lips. Maybe he knew it. Maybe he was working her. Maybe somebody had taught him as well as her mamma had taught her. Back at the table, she had listened while Monk acknowledged the severity of her situation and proposed what he thought was a rational solution. Juno wasn't thinking about rational solutions anymore. She was thinking about how Mitchell's men weren't rational at all, that they would hunt her down anyplace, even Costa Rica, and there wasn't a bus, train, or plane that could get her there anyway. They'd catch her, and they'd take her back to Mitchell. And she would rather die. But Mitchell's men knew they had to bring her back alive. They wouldn't kill her, because Mitchell would kill them. Mitchell owned her, and he was going to make sure she knew it.

The car cut sharply, changing in and out of lanes, and Juno let her fingers drag along the cool glass where the blues and pinks and reds blurred like a watercolor. She imagined herself in the old Vegas of the 1970s, Elvis Vegas, with the old neon signs and the gangsters and the evening gowns. She smiled as she pictured herself in a vintage beaded pantsuit with a Joey Heatherton haircut, maybe on the arm of a casino owner or dancing in a revue. But that wasn't her memory. That was her mother's memory, and Juno knew it didn't end well. She was stronger than that.

But when Monk said, "My friend has the perfect place for you to stay," she had decided neither to believe or not believe him. She nodded. Not at all because she trusted him. She nodded because she understood that she had nowhere else to go. She had a Mafia hand, like Bill said at the table. It was too late to get out. She had to play the cards she was holding.

And there was no point in being ungrateful. She'd lived a life few people could imagine, let alone access. The early months, even years, with Mitchell offered her unlimited possibility. She still gambled, but only for entertainment, and instead of back rooms with full ashtrays and empty beer glasses, she traveled to Monaco or to Dubai on private jets, staying in luxury hotels and rented villas. Even tonight, after her world had gone up in flames, she was flying down the Vegas strip in an expensive sportscar driven by a beautiful man. Everything her mother had expected for her. She had achieved it all. She had beaten men at their own game, so many times that victory had lost its luster. *That's it*, she thought. *I've lost my grit. I got soft. And I'm going to pay for it. But so help me, if I get out alive, I'll make my own way. I'll never depend on a man for money or for safety.*

"Listen, you don't have to tell me if you don't want to, but..."

"Okay. Here's the story: from the time I could count, my mama raised me to grift with cards. As soon as I could stand up, she'd take me to fairs and I'd take money from people all day playing Three Card Monte. Even back then, I knew cheating was wrong, and I knew Mama had gotten broken by cheaters, and I couldn't understand why she wanted me to be one. But I did what she said: I practiced, I learned every game, and I got good at hiding every tell. And I learned to fight, because as soon as I started playing out of my class, I had to defend myself. As long as I was playing in back of gas stations and in trailer parks, the farm boys wouldn't lay a hand on me. But my first tournament at a country club in the city, three bankers in golf shirts tried to get the money back I'd won off them by dragging me off in the dark to the eighteenth green. Well, I got away, and at least one of them will probably never have to have a prostate exam again. I threw their money all over the ground from the eighteenth green to about the sixteenth hole, I guess. I like to think they crawled around in the dark to find it.

"I was sixteen. From then on, any man who put his hands on me either got my permission or a trip to the emergency room. And from then on, I decided something else. I would never grift again. Only fair games. No fixes, no stashed cards. I made it in the poker world straight. It was one thing when I was a little kid. People paid for the show, and they got their money's worth. But a grown-ass woman manipulating the cards? She's just dirty.

"So those men after me are not chasing me because I took them, or anybody else. I don't cheat. I play to win, I'm aggressive, and on a good day, nobody can beat me. But it's skill, patience, and knowledge. Reason. Not luck—don't get me started on luck. I made my own luck. I was doing great, and then I met Mitchell. I let my guard down. I thought he was like me, but he wasn't. He's not like anybody. He's not even, like, a human being. By the time I realized I knew too much about his business, I couldn't get out. Stupid. So I was living this life with Mitchell—the houses, the cars, the insane money. His weird projects. But the one thing I couldn't have was my freedom. I wasn't playing tournaments anymore; I had no money of my own. Everything and nothing. And then one day last week, I called an old friend and got into this tournament. It was going to be my escape. But I know Mitchell won't stop, and he's got all the resources to hound me to the end of the earth. Well, does that answer your question?"

Monk nodded slowly, as he had been the entire time Juno was talking. He flashed her a quick smile before saying, "Thanks for that fascinating story, darling, and I really did want to know whose dog you shot, but first I was just going to ask you your name."

Juno put her head in her hands and groaned. "It's Juno," she said. "My name is Juno."

"This Mitchell guy. Is that his first name or his last name? I'm just asking because I know a lot of people, here in Vegas and back east, and I don't—"

Juno shook her head. "Mitchell is his first name. But you wouldn't know that. You'd have heard of XK3, though, I bet." She looked away from Monk, out the window, as he exhaled deeply.

"Mitchell works for XK3? Oh, wait. Oh no."

"Yeah. Exactly. Oh no. If you want out, I completely—"

Monk pulled the car sharply to the curb and turned directly to face her. "Not a chance," he said, "and let me be clear: I was listening. I heard what you said about cheating. I've done a lot of things myself, and I grew up around a lot of deceit and trickery. I didn't want that kind of life. I told you I would help you, and my word means more to me than anything else. Ask anybody in this town and they'll tell you: Monk's word is gold. I knew something was wrong when you left the table. What good is knowing anybody if they won't help you out when you need it? Besides," Monk paused, holding her chin in his hands, "I wanted to see the eyes behind those dark glasses. And they did not disappoint. A man would go a long way to look good in eyes like these." They held each other's gaze there under the blinking casino lights, Monk noticing that the acute desire he felt for this woman only sharpened with each new facet of herself that she revealed to him. He wanted to feel what it was like to be inside all of that electricity. Juno ached for him to kiss her, but she knotted up inside when she thought about having to leave him tomorrow. This was no time to fall for someone. Anyone. Even if he was the only one for her, the fairy tale. *Figures*, she thought. She could hear her mother's laughter as she lowered her eyes from Monk.

———

Juno startled awake, and it took a moment for reality to return. "I can't decide if I should be complimented or insulted." Monk was kneeling next to her, the passenger door open. Shafts of daylight cast a spotlight on the parking garage walls, illuminating the Caesar's Palace logo. "I'm choosing to be impressed, actually, that you could sleep through the rest of that drive. I had to make a few rounds before Bucky could meet us.

Don't worry. You just keep sleeping. We got you." Someone else was there, because Monk asked him to help. "She's exhausted, haha. Long night."

She remembered leaning on Monk, their footsteps echoing in the parking deck. After that, images came in flashes. Thumping club music was playing in the elevator, lit entirely in blue. A long hallway with crimson carpet and cream-colored walls. *Vegas,* Juno thought. *They don't want you to know what time it is. Vegas is a terrible boyfriend. It offers you everything, and the party goes on forever. It holds up mirror after mirror, and you look so beautiful in all of them. But it distorts, it lies to you. It takes away your control and cuts you off from everything you love, everything that matters. No sunrise. No rest. No affection—only a beautiful illusion, an empty façade to mask a bitter cruelty.* Vegas was the Goddess of Luck, and Juno knew luck was the biggest lie of all, the most misplaced faith, the thing men invented to throw stars in the eyes of the believers. Vegas was a terrible boyfriend, the kind that refused to let go. The city itself hemmed her in, trapping her. She'd have been caught already except for...except for... *But nobody helps you without a price coming due. Isn't that right?*

"Who is she?" He had crisp, pressed shirt sleeves with that laundry iron smell. Even half asleep, Juno noticed his deference to Monk, like the man back at the Wagon Wheel.

"Ah, she's just visiting. Kindergarten teacher from

South Carolina. Got a little bored at the convention, you know."

"Hot kindergarten teacher. Man. So you're just helping the tourist board, giving her the full 'what happens in Vegas' experience."

"She was doing fine on her own with that. Figured we'd fall in love for a couple of days. I'm a little bored myself."

"Bored? You're a riot, man. Bored." Juno found their whispers and laughter almost reassuring. She had met every goal her mother had set for her and she wasn't yet thirty-five. She had bested so many adversaries and survived. Floating into deep sleep in a white cloud that smelled like the air in a French countryside, Juno welcomed the idea that she had nothing left to lose. *Is this what luck feels like?* she thought. Flickering in front of her eyes was the image of Monk Mason Davies kicked back on an elaborate chaise, covered in what looked like a blanket of feathers. Or enormous wings.

"Why are you doing all this for me?" Later, Juno would scarcely remember asking the question. But she remembered Monk's answer forever. He must have thought she was still asleep or he never would have said such a thing. Maybe she was dreaming, or maybe he was.

SEVEN

Morning happened over and over in Las Vegas. Every time somebody woke up, it was morning all over again. The time of day didn't matter. Time wasn't real in Vegas; there were no clocks or open windows. Juno recognized morning in the soft sound of a shower running and the smell of bacon. She opened her eyes.

Wonder wasn't an emotion Juno was accustomed to feeling anymore. It had left her sometime back, along with a collection of sentiments even less useful to a professional gambler. Anything related to surprise had to be collected, neutralized, and eliminated. As Juno started to take in her surroundings, flashes of her childhood came back to her as she experienced the particular thrill of unexpected beauty, especially the private kind, the particular satisfaction of seeing something grand that you believe might just be meant only for you.

First, there was the ceiling itself. Right above her head, fat baby cherubs floated in a shade of blue she'd seen only once or twice, in the skies of the Amalfi coast and on the hills of the Acropolis. They circled into a concentration of wings around a center point, a painted replica of a great dome. Their faces peered down at Juno in the enormous bed, some with wide-eyed innocence and benevolence, some with roguish smirks and leers. Some angels carried baskets of fruits or small animals, lambs and foxes, while others held arrows or grasped for one another. Everything else in the room appeared to be white, silver, or mirrored. In the haze of waking, it all seemed infinite. Here was an afterlife Juno could desire, even hope for.

She didn't want to move and break the spell, but the smells of coffee and bacon drew her to the edge of the bed. Her head was pounding. But set before her on a round table covered in white damask she found a series of shining silver domes of various sizes, along with a massive silver pot, steam rising from its neck. Her hands found the porcelain cup and its saucer, and she managed to down two helpings of coffee before even considering further investigation. She crouched on the edge of the bed, hugging her knees, as she lifted each silver dome. Under one, hardboiled eggs sat upright in painted china egg cups. Another revealed a silver rack of toast, browned to perfection. She bit her lip and lifted another to find enormous strawberries, nearly bursting in their skins, clustered around a ramekin of clotted cream. There was oatmeal with nutmeg, dates, and crisp pecans. Belgian waffles with maple syrup. When she found the bacon, she took a single strip and tasted it: smoky, barely charred, crunchy like it came from her grandmother's cast-iron pan. She peeked under another and found the biggest surprise: biscuits, real ones, like she hadn't seen in years. She seized one, almost as a challenge, only to find it so authentic she could almost hear the chickens in the neighbor's yard and the creak of a screen door.

"I didn't know what you eat for breakfast, I mean, normally. I was hoping to make something normal at least." Freshly showered and dressed simply in a white tee shirt and jeans, Monk leaned against the bedroom doorway. She noticed his eyes still had the little wrinkles around them even when he wasn't smiling, which was rare. Just as handsome with this serious expression, she noted. "I was a little worried about you. You slept a good fourteen hours there. Not that it matters. It's Vegas. Everybody sleeps through the day. And as you can see, you're safe here. Do you need anything? Come on. I'll show you around. It's a big suite. Kind of ridiculous, actually. But I can explain. It'll make sense in a second. You okay?"

Juno nodded, holding a giant strawberry in one hand and clinging to a cup of coffee in the other, waving the strawberry around for emphasis while chewing. She unfolded her legs and hopped from the high bed to the deep white fur rug that lined the bedroom. "Here, you've got a little bit of something..." Monk picked up a cloth from the table and dabbed her cheek before popping one of the strawberries into his mouth.

"The biscuits," Juno mumbled, her mouth still full, pointing to the tray piled high with them.

"Oh yeah? They meet your approval? I'll take one for the trip. It's a big suite. Wait until you see." Monk took Juno's hand and led her across the bedroom threshold. She gasped—not a fake gasp, not a polite gasp, not a reaction she chose in order to make a man feel better or worse about himself. A real expression of shock. By the time Juno had ended up in a penthouse suite with Monk Davies, she had seen all the opulence the world could offer. Nothing prepared her for the splendor she saw. And it wasn't just the richness of the surroundings, the sumptuous carpets, the velvet-flocked wallpaper, the wall of glass that seemed to go on forever. It wasn't just the view—my God, she could see all the way to the desert, the sun spilling red, orange, and purple over a hazy ridge in the distance. There was something so particular about the place. Maybe it was the enormous portrait on the far wall, a beautiful goddess reclining, her arm extended in friendship, her gaze steady, a familiar smile... It looked like...

"Monk, is that Celine Dion?" Juno almost spilled her coffee, to her horror, on the white carpet. She set the cup down and started to giggle. "Oh my God. It's Celine Dion. Are we in Celine Dion's apartment?"

Monk nodded. "Well, sort of. She stays here during her residency. But she's on a European tour for the next month, and my buddy is her assistant here, and so..."

"Oh my God. This is insane. It's so insane. It's really, really crazy...and I just, well. Thank you." Monk smiled, but as Juno moved toward him, he darted ahead.

"Look over here. I'll show you the kitchen. See these panels?" Monk pressed a button by the light switch, and a series of wall sections folded back on one another to reveal a bright kitchen almost entirely of stainless steel, with a glass-front refrigerator and an enormous industrial oven.

"Wow, I thought this place was swanky, but I see there's no room service," Juno quipped.

"Check this out. It wraps around this way." Monk led her past Pre-Raphaelite paintings—Juno didn't look closely to see if they were reproductions—of Dante's Beatrice, Persephone, Helen of Troy. A white baby grand piano anchored the next room, and Monk slid his hand across the keys as they passed it. "Do you play?" he asked Juno.

"That's one thing I don't play." Juno shook her head.

As they rounded the last turn of the 360-degree suite, Juno gasped again at the lap pool, blue and still, lined with an elaborate mosaic of the Nine Muses. "So," Monk began, taking a bite out of the biscuit he'd been carrying around. "Think you can stand it here for a little while? Oh, damn. These biscuits are good. Wow."

"Just like Mama never made." Juno sighed. She could stand it here for a little while. Maybe. What would it cost her? Maybe more than she could offer.

"I was thinking we should go out," Monk said, dusting biscuit crumbs off on his tee shirt. "What do you think?"

What I think, Juno told herself, *is that maybe I'm dead already.* "Why not?" she answered. "I'm only a fugitive from a relentless man with unlimited resources. I may as well hop up on stage with the show-girls at the Crazy Horse." Juno shrugged. "I'm going to need a shower, though."

"Oh, I almost forgot the really fun part." Monk led Juno past several other smaller bedrooms until they made the full circle back to the magnificent room where she had slept. Past the bed chamber and its extraordinary ceiling, Monk showed her the bath suite with its marble soaking tub fed by another cherub statue holding a massive urn to pour the water. The marble shower was approximately the size of Juno's first apartment. Beyond the marble and mosaic, a mahogany swinging door with a porthole opened into a massive closet.

Juno stepped past Monk. "Are these what I think they are?" Rows of sequins, gold and silver lame, white satin and feathers.

"She might be a little taller than you," Monk ventured. "But I bet you can find something that suits you. Pick anything. My friend assures me it's okay. You take your time; I'm going to make some arrangements." Monk kissed her, again on the forehead.

Juno felt a pang. "Don't do that," she said, almost whispering so that Monk leaned close.

"Don't do what?" he whispered, his lips so close.

This time, she stepped away. "Don't feel sorry for me," she said, arching her eyebrows and pulling her mouth sharp.

And then it came again, his warm laugh. "Trust me: the last thing I feel for you is sorry. Catch your breath. Take your time. I'm going to show you a Vegas you haven't seen, and I don't care how many times you've been here. Leave it to me."

EIGHT

Monk left Juno contemplating a halter gown covered entirely in enormous rose gold paillettes. "You're too long, sweetie," Juno whispered to the dress, carefully hanging it back. But she tried on a black ostrich feather mini dress. Feeling a little like a Muppet or a fancy evening bag, she rejected that one, too. In the three-way mirror, she studied herself in a body-hugging lemon-yellow leather corset dress, a red satin off-the-shoulder tea-length ball gown with a circle skirt, and a stunning pair of snakeskin pants with a matching bandeau top. Cashmere wraps, scarves of sheer chiffon, and feather boas in every color hung from hooks around the room. Studying herself in her own black lace lingerie, she tried on a shapely black fedora, pulling it over one eye. From the jewelry cabinet next to the mirror, she withdrew a long chain set with garnets and draped it around her waist and hips. *Maybe I'll wear this, and we'll stay in*, she thought.

"I thought we'd get something to eat—I've made some arrangements; trust me, nobody will see us. I have a couple of friends who can hook us up. But would you like a drink before we— Oh. Oh, wow."

"It's working for me?"

"I should say it is. Are those crystals? Wow; you're like a sexy snowflake."

Juno had found the perfect dress, just as she had been staring at herself in nothing much more than a glamorous hat. She'd noticed a flash in the mirror, a glint from one of the glass beads ornamenting the bias-cut midi wrap dress. The flesh-colored underdress gave the illusion of nudity under a fine silver-white mesh. A velvet scrollwork pattern appeared to cling delicately to her body, covering her breasts and triangle, coiling suggestively across her hip bones. Intricate glass bead-work highlighted every curve of her body. She felt like a chandelier loosed from the ceiling, swinging out on her own.

"Careful, mister. I'm no snowflake."

"I think I'm clear on that. You were taking me to the woodshed in that poker game. Uncle Sal would be ashamed of me. He'd say he taught me better than to let a hot girl distract me and take my money."

"Well, thank Uncle Sal for calling me hot. But I beat you fairly. You might have been a little distracted." *So was I*, Juno thought to herself, but only smiled a little. "And I might have been a little out of practice," she offered instead, "but that table is my home. That's the safest place in the world for me. I know exactly who I am and what I'm doing when I'm there."

Monk tilted his head and squinted, as if he were considering a bluff. "No," he said softly, "now I don't think you're giving yourself enough credit. I saw you stand up to some pretty scary-looking guys like you were both Butch and Sundance. In the body of a goddess." He stood and slid his hands into his pockets, leaning back on his heels. *Every move*, Juno thought, *is like water. He rocks like waves in the ocean, pulling me like an undertow. Like the meander of a big river.* "You're like a superhero," he said, a little bashful. She couldn't tell if he was teasing.

"Right," she said, rolling her eyes. "I'm Danger Girl. Capable of finding the hazard in any room."

"And charming it like a sorceress. Okay, let me think. What's your favorite place to eat around here?" It occurred to Juno that most of the time she'd ever spent in Vegas had been at a poker table.

"You'd think I'd have one, wouldn't you?" She sighed. "I've made a pretty good study of all the room service club sandwiches."

"You seem like a steak girl. What about spicy food? Oh, and we can't miss the oysters... Sorry! It's been a while since I took a superhero to dinner."

"I actually find that hard to believe." Juno put her hand on her hip, and the baubles on her dress jingled a little. It made her laugh.

"Oh, see, that's what I was hoping for." Monk

picked up her hand in his for a second. "A real laugh. You keep those safe, don't you? The real feelings."

Juno twisted her mouth a little, trying to decide how to take that observation. She'd always thought transparency was overrated. A little mystery kept a relationship hot. This guy was a showroom window, but she was finding it charming. Hadn't she had enough mystery? And how had it worked for her? Running from thugs with what she could carry. No one who would report her missing if she couldn't hold them off.

"So, Korean barbecue? Lobster? Maybe we should start with drinks."

"Surprise me," she said, shrugging. "I love surprises."

"Girl, I believe you." Monk offered his arm extravagantly, along with that big, sweet smile. "How do you feel about paella?"

Juno looked him up and down and could find no flaw. "Pretty good," she said. "I feel pretty good about all of those things."

————

"Mooonk! Hey, look who's back, everybody." From the other side of the kitchen line, lanky man in chef's whites waved a spatula at them. A row of white-coated men and women called out to Monk like a chorus over the clanking of sauté pans against stove burners and knives chopping against wooden blocks. He wiped his hands and face while he crossed the bustling kitchen. "So, no corner table tonight?"

"Not tonight, Walt. Juno, meet Walt. This is his place."

"Well, yes, actually, the kitchen is more my place. We usually let the guests eat comfortably in the dining room. It's a strange practice, I know, but so far it's working for us. Juno, we can get you some better ambiance than this. Dude, why are you hiding this glorious woman?"

Juno tried to catch Monk's eye, but he was laughing and talking animatedly to Walt. *Of course*, she thought. Monk wouldn't have told him. That's the whole point, as Monk explained. He was taking her on a secret "behind-the-scenes" tour. Early that evening, they'd been picked up by a circus wagon of a white stretch limousine at the corner of Flamingo Road and Dean Martin Drive. The limo driver—was there no end to Monk's friends—left them at the end of an alley too narrow for the vehicle to navigate. Monk pointed to a ragged metal door, and Juno carefully placed her borrowed Jimmy Choo heels one by one between the trash piles so the silver tassels wouldn't get dirty. Monk's arm swept her across the doorway; in his embrace, she could smell the bergamot and spruce in his cologne blending with the deep, earthy scent of leather. Her cheek barely grazed his, enough to feel the scruff of his beard. Juno hadn't felt desire this deeply in her bones for a long time. Sex was something else she had mastered, something she felt good at. For years, it had been a performance, like her persona at the poker table. She liked surprising men with her adventurousness, her insatiable enthusiasm for their bodies. For her, part of the satisfaction was leaving them guessing, knowing all along it was her own appetite that sated her, not them. They could think what they want, but for Juno, she'd found most men easily replaceable. She couldn't explain why she'd stayed with Mitchell. She'd been under a spell, in the land of the lotus-eaters. The day she woke up, she realized he'd never allow her to go.

Now all she wanted was to sink into Monk's blissful, warm ease. *This*, Juno's inner voice said to her, *is just another spell. Keep your head, girl. And your heart.* But in that pause there in the doorway, Juno wanted nothing more than to stay pressed against Monk's strong frame. *This one is different*, she thought. *Something in him is the same as me. This careless man, with no sense of self preservation. Something is there, and it draws me to him.*

Monk, as if he could sense her thoughts, pulled her closer for an instant, then released her. He took her hand and walked her toward the bright light at the end of the short hallway where laughter and kitchen noises and the smells of cooking reminded her of a home she hadn't seen in a long time.

NINE

That night, they knocked on so many ragged doors in so many alleys. And Monk was greeted the same way in every kitchen across town, with laughter, hugs, jokes, stories—it seemed to Juno like the man knew everybody. That must have been it; he'd been a sous chef or a caterer or something. She could hear her granny's advice: "Never trust a man who is mean to the waitress." Based on the Granny meter, Monk was the most trustworthy man she'd ever meet. He was definitely food service approved. And he knew his way in and out of every service entrance in the city.

Walt had served them two perfectly seared scallops on a bright purple purée: smoky, rich, and velvety. Each kitchen produced a single dish for them to share. They stood right at the end of the long, stainless steel counters in enormous, florescent, industrial kitchens. They sat on barrels in the corner of a tiny, dark kitchen where the two chefs whispered and seemed to be casting spells over piles of vegetables and herbs. Juno watched a Brazilian sous chef juggle knives; a French former showgirl trained as a butcher showed her how to debone a quail. The dishes were as fascinating, sometimes complicated, and as singular as the people she met that night. A savory soup of artichoke and black truffles, served in shot glasses. Slivers of duck breast, crisp Wagyu beef rolls set on salt blocks, sea urchin sushi bites. Miniature blinis dotted with tangy caviar. A flaming baked Alaska shaped like a beehive. A halved lemon with white chocolate spikes, each tipped in gold foil fringe. Chocolate mousse in the shape of a tiny fedora: "Sinatra's hat."

"Oh, I almost wore a hat like this one to dinner." Juno smiled at the memory of looking at herself in the mirror. "Maybe I'll try it on again later. Right now, I can't eat another bite."

"We have another stop." Monk checked his watch. "Two minutes before we rendezvous at the corner! Let's go. Have I mentioned how much I admire your costume? I'll never look at the chandelier in the lobby of the MGM the same way again. Do you take a class for that, or do you just move that way naturally?"

Juno bumped Monk with her hip, and the baubles on her dress rang like tiny bells. "I seriously can't eat anymore, Monk," Juno said, "I loved it. I loved it all, and thank you. It's been a long time since I was in a restaurant kitchen, and I forgot how wonderful it can be. You went to a lot of trouble, and, for a little while at least, I forgot..."

"Good!" Monk cut her off and swung open the metal door. "Let's keep that going. I have another place to take you. No food at this one. Tasting is over; now it's time for a different sense. Touch!" He grinned. "I see that look. Just get in. All will be revealed."

The limo crawled down Las Vegas Boulevard in traffic. Monk saw Juno startle and slump down in the seat when a large, black SUV came to a stop beside them at a traffic light. He reached over and tapped her knee. "Hey, those shoes," he began, "first of all, they're great. I'll admit, high heels do it for me. And those are some sexy high heels. May I?" He tapped her knee again, and Juno turned toward him. She cocked one eyebrow and smirked, slowly raising both feet and placing them next to Monk on the upholstery. Monk nodded slowly, picking up one of her feet to study it closely.

"The thing is," he went on, "while I enjoy them, I wonder. Do you enjoy them?"

"Do I like these shoes? I love these shoes. They're from his 2018 collection. I had a similar pair in— That's not what you mean, is it?"

Monk shook his head slightly. He started to lift the leather strap carefully, loosening it from the buckle. Juno shifted a little, feeling a static charge moving up her leg to her inner thigh. "I mean," Monk said, furrowing his brow into sadness, "your feet have to be killing you. I can't even imagine."

Juno chuckled. "I don't even think about it anymore. Oh, maybe once in a while it's bad. I usually stash a pair of flats in my bag in case it's really bad. Or in case I have to flee." She glanced out the window again but quickly turned back to Monk's face in the soft light of the limo. All the neon was muted by the tint, but they were both bathed in a pinkish glow.

Monk slid the strap from Juno's ankle, gliding his thumb along her instep as he guided the shoe from her foot. Juno sighed, more deeply than she had intended, and Monk smiled. Using both thumbs, he pressed hard into the ball of her foot. "Oh, God," Juno blurted out. Tears came to her eyes. "Do you take some sort of class for *that*? Or did it come to you naturally? Holy— Oh! That's the spot! Oh!"

"See, that's what I like to hear from a woman. So they make your feet hurt, I mean, clearly your feet hurt, but you wear them because...you like how they look. But also because it feels like this when you take them off. I understand." Monk looked away and grew serious for a second. Then, as if to himself, he whispered, "This is why I continue to believe women are fundamentally stronger than men. Okay," he turned to Juno, "other foot. There you go."

Juno realized her mouth was open as she let her other foot drop to the floor of the limo. She moaned again as Monk kneaded her foot. *Is that a thing*, she wondered, *where you start thinking you've already died and you're in some sort of afterlife? Maybe they shot me in the alley. Maybe Mitchell really did strangle me in my bedroom months ago. And I'm wandering the earth until my soul is satisfied.* She looked at Monk and smiled. *I must have worked off some of my sins in the last few weeks. Because this place looks a little better by the hour.*

Monk was explaining something, but she felt so good she could hardly focus on the words. "...so it was important to me, you know, that it be fair. A fair contest. Because in our last competition, you beat me. And as you say, it was fair." He reached under the seat and retrieved her neat little pair of Keds sneakers, the ones she had put on to run from the casino. "I wanted to be certain that the field was even. No uncomfortable shoes, no secret distractions. Well, I'm still going to be a little distracted. What kind of engineering keeps that dress on you? Don't tell me. I want my head clear." Monk placed each sneaker on her feet and tied them. "Too tight? Or just right?"

"Monk, what is happening?"

"I want you comfortable and ready, so that it will be fair and square when I beat you, that's all!" Monk waved a hand, and the back door opened. Juno looked outside. Right across from the Welcome to Las Vegas sign was a building covered with one word.

TEN

"Pinball?"

"Not just 'pinball,' woman! It's the Pinball Hall of Fame! There are about five hundred classic pinball games in that building. I'm high score on, well, some of them. We're having our own private tournament so I can get back some of my dignity I lost at the poker table. That's right, you and me, and I'm going to be bringing it. We can decide on a bet later— Hell, I don't even care if we bet. I want the crown, that's all. Pinball Champion! I'm coming for you. What? You're a pinball girl; I know it. Don't tell me I'm wrong."

"Oh, you're wrong, big time." Juno stepped out of the car and drew herself as tall as she could next to Monk. "You're wrong if you think you can beat me!" She sprinted across the parking lot to the entrance, where a "Closed" sign was still swinging from having been flipped over. Juno spun around to see Monk waving. "Another friend of yours?" Monk shrugged. "Okay, okay. I'm impressed. You know everybody."

"Everybody. And it didn't matter a bit to me, because I hadn't met you, gorgeous, until yesterday."

Juno punched him lightly. "I know what you're up to."

"Is it working?"

"I'm a little distracted, yes."

"Great news!"

"Monk! Look at you. Where have you been keeping yourself? Well, well. That was a stupid question now that I see. Introduce me and make me sound interesting, because I'm sure not good-looking as you."

"Juno, this is Hal. He will be trying to take you away from me for the rest of the evening. Careful with him; he's a poet."

"Welcome, Juno. I've known this outlaw since he was twelve, and I don't think he's going to amount to much. You come see me when you're done with him. Monk, I'm following you around from now on because I want to know where to find women like this."

"She was kicking my ass in a poker game."

"Oh, hell, she's perfect is what you're saying." Hal beamed at both of them. "The place is all yours, kids. Closed up early. Monk, here's the key; you know where to leave it."

Juno scanned the long aisles of flashing pinball machines. "Start wherever you want," Monk called, hanging his jacket on a hook behind the counter.

She ran her hand along the glass and chrome. "Touch," she said, "and I thought you meant the foot massage." She looked back at him. "This place is beautiful."

"I knew you'd love it. Hal retired out here after closing his arcade in Wisconsin. All those years, he saved the old games. He could have rotated them back to the distributor, but the manufacturers would only give the arcade owners fifty bucks for a used machine. It wasn't worth it, so he kept hundreds of them. He had a shed full of these classic games, restored them by hand, one at a time. He used to have parties out at his house, until there were hundreds of people coming."

"Wow. So in retirement, he found a whole new business?"

"Nah. He does it all for charity. And you know. Love."

Monk pulled back the plunger and released it. The machine came to life as the silver ball danced across the playfield and into the bumpers. The bells and sirens sang out. The machine, *Eight Ball Deluxe*, featured a Robert Redford–type cowboy cueing up at a pool table, his hat dipping over his eye. Minus the hat and the bushy moustache, Monk stood like a mirror of the handsome shooter, bent over the pinball machine, working the flippers. His shoulders rolled in waves; his hips rocked against the machine.

"Two can play at this game, you know." Juno folded her arms and watched Monk. He was doing that same seductive dance he was doing at the poker table.

"Actually," Monk said, keeping his eyes on the machine, "this one's a one-player game. The multiplayer games are on the back wall..."

"You know perfectly well what I mean," Juno said, marching over to the machine next to *Eight Ball Deluxe*. The backbox featured a beautiful woman sitting at a poker table full of monsters. She had long, green hair, and she stared out from the panel directly at the player, holding up the Ace of Spades.

"*Asteroid Annie*," Monk said. "One of my childhood favorites. I always thought maybe it was based on the cantina in *Star Wars*. If somehow Lynda Carter had been sitting randomly at one of the tables. Hey, don't forget the start button is—"

"You think I don't know where the start button is? Don't mansplain pinball to me, mister. Annie and me, we go way back." Juno tapped the plunger with the tip of her index finger before pulling it with a snap. The silver ball flew up, landing immediately in the bonus slot.

Monk's laugh was deep and loud, echoing through the empty warehouse. "Okay, okay. I like a challenge. But you're in my house tonight. I'm coming out on top this time."

Juno snorted a little when she laughed. "Don't you ever get tired of the *constant* innuendo?" she groaned, rolling her eyes. "That was bad, even for you."

He was laughing even harder as his ball hit the drain. "Bad, and accidental. Or I've just somehow along the way become the sleazy guy I have so often pretended to be." He stood back from the machine while Juno finished her round. "Zip ball," he sighed. "That better not happen again, or I will not be able to show my face in here."

"I won't tell the other pinheads you let a girl beat you. Come on, Annie." Juno had one ball left, and it would have to be a good one to beat Monk's score.

Monk clapped his hands. "Go, girl. Biff it. Come after me." Juno set the plunger loose, and the backbox lit up as the ball bounced between the popping bumpers. "Yeah, baby! Keep it going!" Juno held back and waited until the ball rolled to the end of the flipper before sending it sailing back into the playfield. All four aces lit up, and she threw her hands in the air, laughing. "She shoots; she scores!" Monk lifted her briefly into the air.

"Why are you celebrating? I beat you!"

"Masterfully, yes! But that was the first round; it's a two out of three tournament."

"Oh, I see! Well, I better find my next machine."

"Choose wisely, youngling. I will play the one next to you. Unless it's *Gilligan's Island*."

"Why? Ginger's too much of a distraction? Or are you about to tell me you're more of a Mary-Anne man?"

"Neither. Now, if the Professor had been a chick..."

They played games she'd never seen: *Cactus Canyon*, *Pirates of the Caribbean*, *The Mandalorian*. Finally, Juno stopped in front of a game called

Haunted House. She touched the chrome thoughtfully.

"This one? A total classic. One of my favorites. We can take turns if you want."

"I used to..." Juno stopped. *What's the point,* she thought, *in hiding anything? Everything is already on the table. I may as well show my hand.* "My brother. I played *Haunted House* with him. Gosh, it looks like the exact same machine. We used to walk up to this little cinderblock convenience store at the entrance to the trailer park. Mama never had any money, but my brother, he always had a few quarters and he'd share with me. We'd get RC Colas and Moon Pies. This is it. I can't believe it. I haven't seen this in ages."

Juno's memories unspooled from the tight knot she'd wound to keep them safe. She could smell the cigarettes and bait for sale behind the counter, the faint odor of kerosene. "It was over in the corner, and I was afraid of it at first. But I couldn't stop looking at it. Jack, though, he was fearless. He was excited. There had been an old, busted pool table that didn't even have all the balls and was missing a foot. One day it was gone, and here was this pinball machine. That woman in the white nightgown standing there in the doorway. I couldn't tell if she was running away or if she was the ghost. I guess when I started playing, she was me." Juno smiled. "I drew that owl on the tree branch on so many school notebooks. So he could watch over..."

Monk watched her face, waiting for the story he somehow knew come. "After Jack disappeared," Juno said, matter-of-factly, "I'd come to the store alone, all the way through high school. Well, until I left. I'd look at the cemetery fence and wonder if he was in the ground someplace, a place I'd never find. I'd look at the attic, the shadowy light, and I'd wonder if he had found a way out. I'd think of him some place like the ones we talked about. New York, London, Paris. In a little attic apartment with a cat and a coffeepot and all the books he could ever read. I pictured him happy, and it helped. Even if some days I pictured him as a ghost."

"Juno, I'm sorry. The last thing I wanted you to find in this place was a bad memory."

Juno turned to Monk and shook her head, her eyes bright with tears. "No, no. It's not a bad memory. These are my best memories. You've reminded me of something. You reminded me I had something of value, at least once in my life. Not a winning hand, not a big jackpot. Real value."

"Jack? You still have Jack. Whatever it is that happened. You keep him inside you, in the upstairs light."

Juno nodded. Then she pulled back the plunger and let it go.

ELEVEN

"Don't feel sorry for me."

"You've got to stop saying that."

"I don't need your pity. I went in with my eyes open, just like I always do."

"And I've told you repeatedly, from the time I saw you sit down at that poker table, my only thought has been, 'That woman is rock solid and needs absolutely none of my nonsense.'"

"And yet..."

"I brought my nonsense. But understand: my nonsense is my best quality. It's all I have to offer. That, and my superior, championship-level pinball skills..."

"You're such a gracious winner."

"You literally just said not to feel sorry for you! Hey, if it's any consolation, I usually don't have to work nearly this hard."

"Are we still talking about pinball?"

Monk laughed as the limo drew to a stop. "You up for one more adventure?"

"Hmm. This feels like a dare."

"Not this time. This one is meant only to delight. The danger is only imaginary here."

"Okay then. I'm intrigued." At the mention of danger, though, Juno's thoughts drifted back to reality. In a few hours, surely no more than a few hours, she'd have to confront it. She'd have to leave, probably without a word or a trace. Monk might know everybody in Vegas, but she doubted this man would have the means or inclination to track her. That would be the end. She was having a lovely little fling, maybe the last for a long while. Maybe that's why it seemed so sweet all of sudden to her. He wasn't special. The circumstances were.

"Oh, there it is," Monk said with a rueful click of his teeth. "I'm wearing you down, I know. And then it comes back, the Juno scowl of disapproval. Listen, if I'm a silly distraction, I'm okay with that. I'll be the silly distraction of all time. It's my superpower. Come on—we've got about ten minutes before showtime."

"Showtime?"

"Follow me!" Once again, Juno placed her hand and her future in Monk's grasp. And once again, she could hear her mother's voice telling her, "Nobody does anything for you for nothing." Who he was, what he wanted—she'd set it all aside, just like she had with Mitchell. For all she knew, Monk could be leading her right to Mitchell. He'd had no success taking her by force; she could absolutely see him being devious enough to send a beautiful messenger to lull and lure her. She could be walking down this bright hallway to her death. Or worse, one of Mitchell's remote compounds where she'd never be seen again. There wouldn't even be anyone left behind to wish she was out there, living with books and a cat and a coffeepot in some apartment in Paris. She'd be buried alive.

"This way," Monk said, looking straight ahead of them. He turned down a ramp that led into a dark tunnel. Two men stood at the entrance. Juno heard the crackle of a walkie talkie.

"Hey," Monk said as he got closer. "I think you guys are expecting us." One of the men tapped his earpiece and nodded. Monk walked past them into the blackness of the tunnel.

Once they had walked a good fifty feet or so, Juno felt her eyes adjust. Pinpoint lights were scattered around the floor; they seemed to be following a line of them. Juno could make out some ropes and gears along the walls, some kind of equipment. There was music, theatrical and ornate, and it was getting louder. A figure appeared next to them, gave them a thumbs-up, then led them through a portal, a kind of hatch. Juno had to duck almost to her knees, but when she stood, she found herself in what seemed to be an elevator with an open top. Above, Juno saw a warm glow, some kind of indirect light. The music reached a crescendo, almost deafening. Monk drew her close, even closer than what seemed necessary for the small space. Then he spoke directly into her ear.

"Don't move. But KEEP. LOOKING. UP."

All at once, light burst above them. Applause and exclamations of delight came from all directions. Juno looked side to side, seeing only pitch black. "UP!" Monk held her even tighter. She turned her head in time to see what she thought to be the high ceiling begin to tilt toward them. As the panel slanted toward vertical, she saw them. At least twenty, maybe thirty people dressed in ornate costumes, all dancing impossibly on the tilting wall. When the panel stopped at ninety degrees to them, the edge just above their heads, the dancers were still leaping, kicking, and cartwheeling. *They must be attached to some kind of harnesses*, Juno thought, until one of the dancers began to fall through the air. He plummeted—it had to be at least two stories high—and Juno screamed as the body, arms and legs windmilling, fell straight toward them. She couldn't hear herself over the audience shouts and the music, now heavy with timpani drums and ecstatic clarinet runs. Just as he was about to fall right on top of her, the dancer twisted himself upright and landed in the elevator box next to them, even brushing slightly against Juno's left side. He tapped a spot on his costume and released a harness that retracted with a whoosh of air, and then he darted away through the hatch.

Juno felt Monk's arms tighten around her. She flung her arms around him as two more dancers landed, the updraft and bounce from the floor nearly taking her breath away. They were all falling now, their golden costumes catching the stage lights and making them look like comets sailing down through the dark. She couldn't hear if it was laughter or something else, but against Monk's ribcage, she could feel his whole body shaking as the dancers dropped into the box two or three at a time, exiting just as fast through the hatch.

The last dancer remained on the vertical plane above them. Her red silk kimono sleeves billowed; her hair fanned out as she kicked and sailed out from the wall, directly over Juno's head. She was close enough to touch, Juno thought; on one pass, Juno could have sworn she heard the dancer's deep inhale, even over the continuous drums. When the dancer reached the wall one last time, she ran straight up, her hair flying behind her. Juno remembered that feeling, her hair lifting off her next as she rode behind Jack on his bicycle, almost flying as he took the hills with no brakes. Tears filled her eyes when the dancer, reaching the top edge of the wall, opened her arms and fell backward, tumbling head over heels, as if she'd been shot with an arrow.

The dancer landed next to Juno, vibrating the floor and walls of the enclosure. Unlike the other performers, the woman met Juno's eyes and smiled broadly. Her face had been paper-white, her green eyes outlined with black comma shapes. Jewels shined from her forehead. The elevator filled with the smell of ambergris and oranges as the dancer kissed Juno lightly on the cheek before exiting through the hatch.

TWELVE

The show went on for about two hours, including a fifteen-minute intermission, during which Juno could not stop laughing, mostly at Monk's facial expression when she blurted out, "I thought I was going to die!" first thing when the lights came up. Finally, he started to laugh, too. But they never let go of each other.

The story unfolded above them: two warriors from opposing families become lovers in secret, stealing away to find each other in the shadows. When inevitably they meet on the battlefield, their identities hidden behind their war masks, they don't recognize each other until one is mortally wounded. Discovering she has killed her beloved, the remaining warrior kills herself beside him as both armies stop fighting at the spectacle. The gods, pitying the lovers, descend from the heavens to punish the warring families and to turn the lovers into mythical birds. They must circle the earth forever for their previous sins, but their extraordinary love earns them the right to stay together for eternity. Monk didn't say a word on the limo ride back to Caesar's Palace, only let his arm rest across Juno's shoulders as she settled her head against his chest. Juno kept quiet herself, only whispering "thank you" once. She wasn't sure if Monk heard, but a few minutes later, he kissed the top of her head once again. Juno fought the urge to offer her lips instead. Maybe he did feel a brotherly kind of affection for her, that was all. A grifter helping another grifter. She'd learned that the hustle had no code, no moral imperative. But there were those solitary souls who believed in luck, who believed that helping a kindred spirit would bring a reward.

Through the now-familiar service entrance and up the freight elevator, Juno held Monk's hand but avoided his eyes. She excused herself immediately when they arrived at their suite.

"Wash it off," she said to herself in the mirror. "You just need a long shower and a rest. Don't second-guess the universe that sent you help when you needed it. He's not asking anything; he's just running his own game. Maybe he's atoning for something in his own past. You don't know him." She patted her cheeks and tried to smile at herself. The world, she knew, was full of gorgeous men. Rich ones, poor ones, some clever, some dumb as a box of hair. She could have her old life back soon, with a little patience. *It's for the best, really, if he's not all that interested.* "It's just a game," she whispered, smiling again at herself, ignoring the glistening in her eyes.

Juno undressed with care, replacing the gossamer slip of a dress to its padded, silken hanger. "Best girlfriend," she said to the garment. "Let's hang out again sometime. Hang out, ha ha." Juno cocked her hip to the side. "You're a dress, and I said 'hang out.' Oh, mercy. I need to sleep." She walked into the marble shower and turned on the cold water, as hard as she could stand. The water felt good, and she started to feel like herself again, the good and the bad. She'd been in worse scrapes and survived. Well, bad scrapes. She knew this one might be the worst, but she was ready to face it. She knew who she was, she said to herself. She knew what she wanted.

Dripping from the shower, she found a stack of plush, white hotel robes in the bathroom closet. Wrapping herself in that softness, she heard piano music coming from outside. She didn't recognize the tune, but it spoke to her, melancholy and thoughtful. She wandered over to the bedroom door and listened closely. When she turned the handle slowly and edged the door ajar, she saw Monk. Across that grand room, past the wall of glass that revealed the lights of Vegas as they spread out into the desert, he sat at the enormous white piano. His head hung down close to the keys; his long, nimble hands caressed the keys. *Who are you?* she thought. Juno straightened her spine and pulled the door open. *I may not know who you are. But I know who I am.* She started across the room, whispering to herself, *And I know what I want.*

Monk saw Juno crossing the room. He stopped the song and moved his hands to his thighs, as if he was about to stand. "Don't stop," Juno said softly. "Please."

Monk placed his hands back on the keys, hesitating. He looked up at the big portrait of Celine Dion smiling down at them, raised his eyebrows, and bent over the keys again, his hair falling along his smooth cheekbones. This time, Juno recognized the tune immediately. She matched her steps to each measure, and as the melody reached the chorus, she started to sing the words in a low voice with a clarity of tone that almost surprised Monk. "When you touch me like this, and when you hold me like that..."

Juno touched the side of the piano and slid her hand along its glossy curve as she sang, "I just have to admit that it's all coming back to me." Finally next to Monk, she placed a hand on his shoulder and moved behind him. With her other hand, singing, "When I touch you like this," she reached around Monk's waist and untucked his shirt. "And I hold you like that," she sang softer, unbuttoning his shirt from the bottom. Her hands moved to his ribs, and she felt his breath draw in. Monk spun around on the piano bench and reached for the tie at her waist, but Juno had already flung the bathrobe aside. *If I die tomorrow*, Juno thought, *I'll fly over these lights and remember tonight forever.*

He pulled her hips forward, planting his lips just above her navel. Juno felt liberated, naked in front of the enormous windows, in front of Monk, his tongue moving up her sternum as she eased down to his lap. She had to steady herself on the piano keys as his mouth found her breast, his tongue flicking across the nipple until she let out a shriek of delight. Monk threw back his head, the edges of his soft hair grazing her breasts, which he took into his hands with a moan. She could feel him hard beneath her as she rocked on top of him.

Monk slid his hands down her sides to her hip bones, pushing her harder into his erection. As his hands moved behind her, inside her thighs, she shrieked again. He licked her nipple, then nipped at it gently. "Careful," she said. "I can climax that way. Not yet."

Monk stood up from the bench with Juno wrapped around him. He carried her to the fur rug right in the middle of the wall of windows and laid her down, standing above her to look at her in full view. Juno arched her back against the soft prickles of the fur, feeling it touching her everywhere. She reached her arms over her head, then touched her own nipples, crying out in ecstasy. Monk shrugged out of his unbuttoned shirt and dropped to his knees. Juno snatched his belt loose, staring into his eyes. "Don't feel sorry for me," he said, "or grateful. Or anything boring like that."

Juno stopped him, covering his mouth with a deep, long kiss. It was the way he had kissed her in the casino only a day ago, but this time, what had turned her insides warm and electric before now caused a fire that spread throughout her limbs. Monk swept her up with one arm around her waist and the other hand holding her face close. He kissed her cheek, her ear, her neck, her collarbone. He leaned her back on the rug and again cupped her breast with his hands as he kissed his way down her body.

Her hands settled in his hair, his silky, thick, golden locks. She loved the way it felt against her skin, but she wanted his mouth again. She pulled him up toward her and he lowered his entire body onto hers, kissing her with complete abandon. The pressure of his hip bones and his erection sent her; she grabbed onto his hips with both hands and reached around to hold that gorgeous ass at last. When she could stand it no longer, she tilted her hips and he was inside her immediately, deep and stiff, and her body closed around him. He pulled all the way back and paused before slowly entering her again, his hips slightly swaying and bucking with pleasure. He thrust even deeper; she lifted her hips and squirmed against him, feeling the tickle beginning inside her. She arched her back and he bit down on her nipple. She felt the sensation in waves, as if everything emanating from her body was made of pure light. She hung onto him as the waves continued and seemed to lift her off the ground. Just as she felt she had become the brightest, hottest exploding star, Monk began to moan softly, and she ascended even higher. Her thighs flexed against his surging hips as he called out names of God as if speaking in tongues. They collapsed, spent and sated, into the white cloud of the rug above the sparkling lights below.

THIRTEEN

There was another sound that brought morning to Vegas at any time of the day: a wakeup call. Sometimes it was an alarm you'd set for yourself. Sometimes it was an actual ringing phone. It was why you saw fewer people checking their phones in Vegas. No clocks, no messages, no reminders. All of those things brought the outside world into the fantasy, and nobody wanted that. Not the casinos, not the tourists, not the players, the hustlers, or the outlaws.

Juno had no desire to leave the cocoon of Monk's arms, the rug, the blankets. She didn't care what time it was, even though she had some idea. She'd watched the sun come up through the glass wall, its first rays coming from across the desert tentatively, as if testing to find the best moment to rise. Little shafts of blue first, then pink, until the gold spilled over the horizon and poured into the streets below.

When Juno decided she needed to rise herself, she

moved slowly, too. She untucked her shoulder from Monk's like she was taking apart a puzzle. Once she curled to the edge of the rug, she rolled herself up, allowing the sunlight to cover her skin. She stood for a while there facing her faint reflection in the glass, touching her body with affection, remembering every caress and kiss from hours before. She glanced at Monk, his tanned leg thrown out of the blanket, the curve of his contrastingly pale buttock just visible. She considered lying down again, running her hands and her mouth up his majestic thigh.

Content to imagine that later adventure, Juno padded off to the bathroom, then to the kitchen to search for a little coffee. She picked up Monk's shirt from the floor and reached her arms into it, letting its soft cotton settle across her shoulders. His scent enveloped her again, and her body reacted with excitement. She looked again at him sleeping soundly, sprawled out, arms akimbo. Maybe it was habit; maybe it was a feeling of normalcy she had allowed to settle in, but she reached for her bag on the counter and pulled out the burner phone she'd bought the day before. She even laughed at herself for checking it. There would be no messages; nobody who knew her had the number. She wasn't even sure what the number was. Maybe she should figure that out and give it to Monk, in case she needed to step out. They couldn't stay together all the time. *People don't do that, do they? One day,* she thought, *I won't need a bodyguard. This has to end somehow. Mitchell will get bored. He'll find something else to be angry about, another villain, another person to hound.* She'd seen him do it a million times.

But there was a message, a single text message. *Probably a marketing message from the manufacturer,* Juno thought, breathing a sigh of relief after the shock of seeing the red bubble on the screen. *That'll get better*, she told herself. *I won't jump at every black car, every man with an ear piece, every phone notification.*

The message was one word: *Ramps.* Juno dropped the phone, then stared at it lying there on the marble tile. Monk woke up to find her frozen. When he called out to her, she didn't move or speak. As he came to her, he followed her gaze to the floor.

"Is that phone yours? Didn't you throw your phone out the window."

Juno found her voice. "I did. This one isn't mine. I mean, it's mine; I bought it yesterday at the convenience store when we stopped to get water and ended up with ice cream sandwiches, some Zingers, and those roses."

"And the penguin flashlight."

"And the penguin flashlight, yes. I think you got some flipflops? Anyway, I got the phone, because... I don't know. I thought I might need to get a bus ticket or... I really don't know. I didn't exactly have a plan then."

"Yeah, I get that." Monk was nodding while she talked. "You probably needed to let somebody know, you know. That you're okay. You're okay, right?"

Juno flung her arms around Monk. "I don't want

to go," she said, but her words were muffled as she buried her face in his chest.

"Hey, hey." Monk smoothed her hair and rocked her back and forth. "I don't want you to go, either. What's happening, Juno? Catch me up here."

She leaned down slowly and picked up the phone with two fingers, holding it up to Monk. He took it and looked at the screen.

"It says 'Ramps.' I've seen a lot of threats, but this one is new to me."

"See, that's just the thing," Juno began. "I *don't* have anybody to tell that I'm okay. These last years with Mitchell—I've been cut off from everybody. It's not like I had a lot of friends—"

"Don't say it. Not feeling sorry." Monk held up his hand. "Despite what you may think, given the last days or so, I don't really have a lot of friends, either. Not sure who would know if I walked away for a few days. I mean, nobody. For the most part. My mom might start wondering after a week of unanswered texts."

"That's...adorable, and I wish I could say more about that right now." Juno paused, holding her forehead in both hands. "So, ramps. Mitchell and I were having dinner. It was a gala, actually. Mitchell was being presented with an award for his philanthropy— which is the biggest joke. He donates to his own foundations and siphons the money back into his businesses. It's essentially money laundering, but that's beside the point here, and it's actually not at the top of the list of his most heinous sins." Juno picked up a glass and poured herself some water, then went on. "I remember the night really well for so many reasons. Anyway, it was an elegant situation; there was an embossed, personalized menu card at each place setting. All eight courses described with all their ingredients, the accompanying wine, its vintage, the name of the goat who they milked to make the cheese that went with the figs that were grown on a hill on some Mediterranean island...you know. Excruciating detail.

"Somebody sitting near us was reading the card and having a little fun with it. He was saying things like, 'I don't get the free-range thing. Isn't it worse that the chicken had a happy life?' You know, stuff like that. And then I hear him blurt out, 'Ramps! What the hell? That's not even a food. Ramps?' And Mitchell, who normally didn't often enter casual discussions in the first place, decided to answer him.

"Mitchell said, 'It's clearly a misprint. They overspent on these ridiculous, pretentious menus when we're all having the same dinner. I know what I'm eating; I don't need to be told like I'm a toddler. Then they couldn't even proofread them. It's probably rambutans. Some kind of autocorrect mishap. Sloppy. No excuse.' And he threw the card on the floor. To this day, I don't think it was about the menu card. He was angry already, and the menu card, the other guest, and I ended up on the wrong end of something we had nothing to do with. I should have known better than to say a word.

"But I did. I said, 'Oh, ramps grow wild where I'm

from. More toward the mountains, but I ate them growing up. They're kind of like an onion.' Well, it's true. But sometimes the truth isn't the point, you know? But wait, that wasn't even the end of it. Maybe if it had stopped there, but it didn't."

FOURTEEN

Monk listened to Juno tell this story, nodding occasionally, and only breaking eye contact long enough to make a pot of coffee. He tried not to interrupt, though he feared he knew exactly where they were headed.

"So, a graceful retraction was not going to be an option. When Mitchell did the thing he usually did, dismissing anything I had to say with this little exhale he did—I don't think he knew how silly he sounded; I wish I had recorded him—anyway, he'd puff and push his breath out like a porpoise, which he did. Puff, pop. 'That's inaccurate,' he said. 'You are confused. You are thinking of something else. There's no onion-like thing called a ramp. Don't be ridiculous.' It turned out the chef himself, unfortunately for me, had come out to shake hands with Mitchell and to ask if he had any dietary issues with anything on the menu. In a colossal case of misreading the room, the chef laughed at him.

'Noooo,' he said, really loudly, so people turned around to see what was happening. 'She's absolutely correct. How fortunate to have grown up where they grow right out of the ground; we have to import them, and they are very sought after right now.' And see, I was still clueless. To the chef, I said, 'Oh, right. We were fortunate. We couldn't afford name brand cereal, but we could eat up a big bowl of ramps any old time.' The chef, he had a sense of humor, and we ended up laughing about how if my granny was still alive, she'd FedEx him a box of ramps, even if she'd think this big city chef must be nuts.

"So as we're having a big time, I realize Mitchell isn't looking. At anything. Not at me, not at the chef, not at the guy who started this whole mess. Not at the menu card on the floor. He's tapping his fork on the table, staring out across the room at nothing." Monk put his coffee cup down and stood up. He seemed not to know what to do with his hands, running them through his hair until he placed them on the kitchen counter as if to hold himself up.

"We get through the dinner in silence, mostly. I thought maybe the whole thing would blow over. Mitchell asked me if I wanted to stay in the apartment in the city that night or take the car out to the house. Which I did think was strange. Normally, he'd just say, 'We're taking the car out to the house' or, 'We're staying at the apartment tonight.' I couldn't tell, exactly. He made a short speech about space travel when he accepted the award, a little story about wanting to be an astronaut when he was a boy. It was a speech I'd heard him make before, but I clapped and smiled like his fan boys always do. No matter what the occasion, when Mitchell appears as XK3, he's talking to his followers, and there are certain things they expect. The promise of space travel, the colony they want to have one day. I know." Juno saw the look on Monk's face. "I know. I knew it then, but it seemed mostly harmless. I can't believe I'm saying that now. But remember, this was a few years ago. Before the stories in the press.

"I'm getting to the part that matters now. When Mitchell asked, I said I'd like to stay in the city. It wasn't a big deal, but it seemed practical to me, instead of driving all the way to Connecticut after the gala. When we got in the car, that was my first indication of what was to come. Mitchell told the driver, 'We're staying at the house tonight instead of the apartment. Close the window, please.' He hit me the first time just as the compartment window closed. I think I might have been unconscious for a bit, because the next thing I remember—" Juno paused, taking a deep breath. "The next thing I remember, he was on top of me, holding me down by the throat with one hand. His other hand was drawn back in a fist, and he was screaming something I couldn't understand. It sounded like gibberish. Like when I went to my crazy aunt's church and they spoke in tongues.

"Maybe I didn't get knocked out and I've just blocked it. I remember flashes. I hurt everywhere the next day, but the bruises were small. I had some small cuts I didn't even remember. You know, I went to get an x-ray one time to make sure he hadn't put a chip in me? That's when you know the relationship is over, by the way. When you have to get a medical professional to show you that you do not have a tracking device in your thigh.

"So, yeah. That was a terrible night. But honestly, what happened later was worse. I was shopping in Milan one afternoon, a few months later. I'd been to La Rinascente, and I was picking up some shoes I'd ordered for Mitchell from Belfiore so he might stop wearing those god-awful beige sneakers. I stopped to get an espresso and to sit for a minute. I rarely got to be alone, so sitting in a café for a minute while I was out shopping was like a mental health moment for me. Of course Mitchell's men, my bodyguards, were trailing along, but I was used to them by then. I heard my phone message tone, so I looked. It was just the word 'Ramps.'

"It came back, parts I'd forgotten or blocked. Sitting in the sunshine among strangers, I felt ripped open and humiliated. I know; it's just a word. But I remembered him saying to me, 'You will never embarrass me again.' And I'll admit, even as he was beating me, I felt powerful. I embarrassed him in front of people. I'd never seen him second-guess himself on a single thing. Mitchell believes he is superior to other human beings in all ways. He thinks he is a beacon, a herald of some new life form or something. But somehow, the fact that he didn't know what a ramp was and I did, that concept had completely thrown him.

Juno held up a finger to Monk, watching his face again. "I know it wasn't just that I knew something he didn't. I know it was that a stranger sided with me." She nodded and took a sip of coffee. "It undermined everything. His beliefs, his plans. Someone doubted his authority. Because of me. So his whole focus became making sure that never happened again.

"It's not like he wasn't watching me before, but from then on, I was under constant surveillance. And I would get those messages, the one word. The moment I'd forget for a second. I'd be having a coffee, watching a movie. Doing yoga. I'd be showering. There was no place, he was telling me, no place I could escape him. You know, for the longest time, I thought he was texting me the message each time, like we had some psychic link. It turned out he just set a reminder in my phone." Juno laughed, high and joyless. "I shut off the reminder, of course. But he'd just set it again. The man lives in the virtual world. He's everywhere. I shouldn't have been surprised to see that message. That message will follow me until I die."

Monk picked up the phone again, looked at it, then set it back on the counter. "That's not going to happen," he said calmly. "That is not how this is going to go."

FIFTEEN

"I agree, it's a little chilling that it showed up on this phone you haven't used to contact anybody you know or to interact with any of your accounts. I can't explain it, but it doesn't matter. He might have sent 'ramps' to every burner phone sold in Nevada this week."

"That would certainly make for some interesting conversations out there."

"I wasn't sure about suggesting this before, but now I am. Juno, I can be a bit more helpful than I have been."

"Monk, I might have to sit down for this, because I can't imagine what you've got up your sleeve after securing me in the Celine Dion Fortress of Fabulousness. And giving me the behind-the-scenes epic tour. I'll never be able to thank you enough for helping me remember who I am. That I'm nobody's shadow or muse or captive. I'm not a fugitive. I'm not afraid."

"As inspiring as that idea is, you might want to think about keeping the fugitive thing up, at least until you have a plan. I think you're right, for what it's worth. You scare him. And your freedom is in that, somehow. In the meantime, you need to get out of here. Not here, like, this hotel. I mean Vegas. We," Monk pointed back and forth between himself and Juno, "we are going to get you out of Vegas. Safely."

"I'm wondering if a bus—"

"Juno."

"Oh, wait. Let me guess. Monk, does literally every person in Vegas owe you a favor?"

"There's a story, but it's long, and I'd rather tell it someplace else."

———

"I'm not doing a D.B. Cooper..."

"No, no. No jumps. He lets me... He's got a private jet he keeps in the hangar. I mean, why fly coach if you have a skydiving company, right?"

"I'll take your word for it. Oh, wait. One question."

Juno hadn't asked anything when Monk's friend in the parking garage had waved as they sped past him on a Ducati Streetfighter Monk just seemed to find waiting at the elevator. She hadn't asked when they rode out of town, past smaller and smaller houses with bigger and bigger gaps between them until there seemed to be no buildings at all, just the desert stretching in all directions with the occasional shape on the horizon that might be a car or a building or a municipal airfield, as it happened.

"Sure, sure!"

"Where?" Juno said, shaking her hair out after removing the helmet. "Where are we going?"

Monk nodded slowly, rubbing his chin. "How do you feel about heading back east for a little bit?"

"I don't know," Juno ventured, with just a little bit of a smile. She noticed something new in Monk: a discomfort that had its own charm. "How do *you* feel about heading back east?"

The jet's interior featured camel-colored leather club chairs, a small bar, and two twin beds tucked into private alcoves. "Short trip, Mr. Davies?" The pilot smiled at Monk, but Monk didn't answer immediately. "I meant, uh, no luggage..."

"It's okay, Alan," Monk sighed. "Every trip east is a long trip. Luggage or not."

"We'll keep it safe and smooth for you," Pilot Alan replied, as if he was reassuring an entire commuter flight of restless businessmen. "Refuel in Cincinnati, then on to destination."

"Yes. Destination," Juno said, curling up into a chair and covering herself with one of the plush throws folded in the seats. "Wherever that might be. Do these things recline?" She squinted at Monk.

"There's a little button, I think—check the left side." Monk opened and closed a few compartment doors until he found a couple of pillows and bottles of water.

"Nice plane you've got here," Juno said, studying him.

"Thanks. I mean, yeah. Isn't it? It's pretty slick. My buddy, he rents it out. Lately he mostly uses it for those Life Flight missions." He offered Juno a pillow and a water before settling into the chair across from her. "Stretch out if you want. We'll be up here a while. By the way, you ditched that phone?"

"It's in pieces across some of the least scenic parts of Clark County."

"Good, good. I don't care what kind of surveillance he's got on you, there's no way he'll guess where you're headed."

"I'm on tenterhooks myself."

"Don't get excited."

"Oh, I'm excited."

"I mean, the whole appeal of the place is that there is no action there whatsoever."

"And that's why you left?"

"Mmm. A little bit of that, yes." Monk stared out the window. He broke open his water and drank deeply, almost emptying the bottle in one gulp.

"Let me tell you something." Juno leaned forward across the little glass cocktail table that separated them. Monk smiled and leaned forward, too. "Here's what I know. Every place, no matter how small, boring, or provincial it might seem, has action. I know some little towns with nothing but action. Not much to do but make trouble. So, mister. Let's go see the trouble you left behind. It can't be any worse than mine, as we already know."

Monk leaned his forehead against Juno's. She brushed his hair softly with her hand. "Monk," she whispered. He leaned his head onto her shoulder, and she embraced him. "This plane. It's your plane, isn't it? Just to be clear." Monk let out a muffled, high-pitched groan. "Okay," Juno said, patting his back. "Okay, mister. We've got a long plane ride during which you can tell me who you really are."

This time it was Monk who slept. All the way to Cincinnati, Monk lay with his head in Juno's lap, snoring like a Basset Hound. Juno found it consoling to locate at least one inelegant trait in the man. It was spectacular, actually. He stammered and whimpered in his sleep, then drooled considerably into her lap once he settled down. "Don't worry," she whispered to him. "I'm very good at secrets."

Who is this guy? Juno had been avoiding this question since they met. She'd realized almost immediately that there was more to his story. It wasn't just the network of people and places he seemed to have at the ready, his connections spanning every corner of Las Vegas. Juno had spent a lot of time around powerful people. Monk didn't act like any of them, that much was true. He was goofy, funny, and deeply affectionate. It wasn't his behavior that gave him away. It was the way other people acted around him, and that was a kind of behavior Juno could identify immediately. The slight deference. The desire to please. He could be the greatest, most beloved guy in the whole world, and the tone would be slightly different. People wanted something from him: at a minimum, his approval.

And Monk generously approved. She'd watched him extend himself to every service worker, from Uber drivers to bartenders to pit bosses. Doormen and valets. Cocktail waitresses to ticket takers. He treated them all with dignity and a kind of equality that almost, almost made him seem like one of them. His transparency, she knew, had to be an act. But there was a kind of sincerity, despite the fact that both of them had to realize he was not telling Juno his whole story. Somewhere over the Midwest, in the middle of a clear, bright sky, Juno decided it didn't matter to her. She accepted whatever story was coming.

Sixteen

"Oh, that's just lovely. I'm so sorry." Monk raised his shaggy head and wiped the drool from the corner of his sleepy mouth. *Still sexy*, Juno thought. *I'm sunk.* "So smooth. Very attractive. How's this date going so far? Enough drool? I think I have more. Later I'll, I don't know, belch or sneeze on you."

"Something to look forward to." Juno chuckled, tossing Monk a box of travel tissues. "This plane has everything! I went through all the cabinets while you were sleeping looking for your box of passports and secret weapons."

Monk almost looked authentically surprised. But he recovered quicky. "Did you find the handcuffs?" he asked slyly.

Juno smirked and raised an eyebrow. "No, but I found a package of Zingers so old it still has Snoopy on it. Tell your friend he needs to clean more or eat more. Or both."

"Zingers never go bad. Too many chemicals. Mmm. Where is that package? I could use a snack."

"Can we get something in the airport?" Juno raised the blind and looked out at the tarmac. "Oh, I guess it's not *that* Cincinnati airport. I should have seen that coming."

"Afraid not," Monk said through a mouthful of sponge cake. "There's a pretty sweet vending machine by the back entrance, though."

"Full of ancient Zingers?"

Monk licked his fingers and removed another cake from the package. "Don't knock 'em, as they say..."

"I'll pass. I'll wait for... Where was that you said we were going?"

"I didn't," Monk said, dropping back into the chair across from Juno. "And I'm sorry; I was teasing, and then I fell asleep, and now it's kind of needlessly dramatic. We're going to Vermont. I'm actually... Vermont is actually where I'm from."

Juno sat back. "Monk, I'm genuinely surprised. Vermont was not on the short list of places I thought you might be from." *Then again*, she thought, *what do I even know about you?* But she felt her doubt melting away. The fast-car-driving, fast-talking prince of Vegas was from picturesque Vermont. Her ID Channel nightmare was turning into Hallmark Classic.

Pilot Alan returned, carrying a padded cooler and a hamper. Monk clapped his hands in joy.

"Perfect timing! Juno, you're going to love a three-way. I can't get enough of them. Alan, did you remember the oyster crackers?"

Pilot Alan saw Juno's jaw drop to her knees and waved his hand, laughing. "A three-way, in Cincinnati at least, means a big bowl of pasta with some extraordinary chili from Skyline. And yes," he turned to Monk, "oyster crackers in the bag. Graeter's black raspberry in the cooler, along with a sparkling rose, because, I'm sorry, that will go with your menu here better than what you selected. I took the liberty. Let me get my box of doughnuts and I'll get us back in the air shortly. Holtman's—Juno, I can tell by your response here that you haven't been to the area before. Take one of these before I go, trust me."

Juno walked around staring at the large doughnut in her hand while Monk set out everything from the bag out on the table: steaming bowls of pasta topped with chili and a mountain of cheese. Even more appetizing, thought Juno, was that dance again. She watched his behind as it swayed.

"By the way, I'm lactose intolerant," she pronounced, hands on hips. Then she imitated Monk's trademark moves, circling her hips like a dashboard hula dancer.

"Oh, man. You almost got me. But see, I knew that wasn't true." Monk shook his finger. "I saw you pounce on Suzanne's profiteroles."

"Why does everything sound so, so dirty when you say it?"

"Maybe you're disappointed in a three-way that only involves chili?"

"Ah, I'm not your girl on that count. Sorry."

"Don't be," Monk said, drawing her close. "You didn't really think I'd share you with Pilot Alan? I mean, he's cute, but..." Juno kissed him, lightly but long. His lips were salty and sweet. She slipped her fingers into his hair and found the curve his head down to his neck. She leaned back and gazed at him.

"One question," Juno said, her brow wrinkled in thought. "About Vermont. Will I have to wear one of those sweaters?"

On the takeoff from Cincinnati, Juno sat in the co-pilot's seat. She'd been on private planes before, even once or twice sitting in front. Mitchell had a pilot's license, of course, because Mitchell believed there wasn't any process he couldn't improve with his own presence. His arrogance made him a dangerous pilot, but his earnest desire to conquer Juno's fear had actually helped her. Now that she understood the physics and the engineering, she found the takeoffs that used to terrify her now filled her with wonder and awe. It was all about knowing what was real, Juno thought to herself. As long as she knew what was true, and where to hold on, she was ready to fly.

SEVENTEEN

The dark four-poster bed was hung with plaid curtains at each corner, like a room within the room. Just beyond, she could see light pouring in through a big bay window, its sill crowded with lush plants and some watering cans. On first waking up, Juno forgot everything; the room reminded her of a story or a movie she couldn't place. It was as if she had gone back to being eighteen, the world spread out around her in all directions, full of possibility. A book, it was a book, she thought. About a family so different from her own. She was waking up in the book, safe from trouble and fear. That's right, she was in Vermont. Monk's home.

She smiled and rolled over in the big bed. *He must have gone downstairs, that's right.* She snuggled back down into the featherbed, into the crisp white sheets that still smelled like him. She could stay as long as she wanted. Time didn't matter, didn't mean anything.

Not like Vegas, where you had to ignore time, pretend it didn't exist so that you could live a fantasy. But here, Juno felt like the weight of time lifted from her like it hadn't since she'd picked up a deck of cards. She couldn't imagine what would make her leave the embrace of this marvelous bed. Then she heard his laugh coming up through the floor, and it felt like Christmas morning.

She hopped off the edge of the high bed feeling like the girl in "The Princess and the Pea." Shearling slippers and a flannel robe lay on a glossy black rocking chair in the corner. Juno put them on and made her way down the steep, wood-paneled staircase, the smells of cedar and coffee wrapping around her. At the landing turn, she could hear two hushed voices.

"There she is." Monk smiled, and Juno felt herself smile without trying. Another old, faintly familiar feeling. The bottom floor was a bar—that's right, she remembered that from their arrival late last night. A pub with a long, ancient wooden bar. Monk was leaning on his elbows, holding a thick mug with "Davies Tavern" in red script. Next to him sat a woman with the same mug and the same sly smile. "Juno, Mom. Mom, Juno."

"Get the poor thing some coffee," the woman said, nudging Monk's shoulder. "I hope you slept well. We used to live upstairs, but now we rent it out during skiing season."

"It's beautiful. Slept like a dream, thank you. It reminds me of a place..."

"You've been to Vermont before?" The woman looked so much like Monk; even the laugh lines around her eyes were shaped like his.

"Never." Juno shook her head, looking at the framed photos that lined the wall all the way to the bar. Most of the photos were of people at the bar itself, some at least a hundred years old. One photo showed the bar packed with people celebrating the end of Prohibition.

"Gloria," the woman said, leaning forward. Juno stared blankly for a second and then laughed, holding out her hand.

"What? I thought my introduction was great. Succinct, heartfelt." He handed another Davies Tavern mug to Juno.

"Knowing how she takes her coffee is a very good start. I'm impressed, Monk."

"Well, she takes it black, just like you. So I don't get to show off my latte art."

Monk's mother Gloria rolled her eyes. "How can you stand it?" she said, winking at Juno. "Monk, I'm going to start the soup for lunch. You know where the food is when you're ready. Juno, we're glad to have you. Our home is your home. If he can't find what you need, find me. And you can stay as long as you like, in case he hasn't told you already."

"Thank you, Gloria." Juno watched Gloria as she walked the length of the bar, polishing with a towel as she went. "Gloria?" she called out, and Monk's mother turned around. "What kind of soup?"

"It's Tuesday, so potato. Want to peel?"

"Very much," Juno said.

"You do not have to peel potatoes," Monk whispered into her ear.

"What if I want to peel potatoes?" Juno whispered back.

"Well, I was thinking I'd take you up to Mount Snow and we could snowboard a little, maybe come back in time for dinner at Chez Milou..."

"Oh, that does sound delightful. I have something I've really, really been wanting to do, though, first," Juno purred.

"Oh yeah?" Monk replied, pulling her closer.

"Yes, yes. Something I can't wait to do, really." Monk laughed low, and Juno whispered, her lips just grazing his cheek, "I...want...to peel potatoes with your mom. And then we can go do whatever you want." She kissed him on the cheek and skipped back to the kitchen.

"Don't talk about me," Monk called after her, half-heartedly. Because he knew well enough.

Eighteen

"That's right. But we only lived here when Monk was a baby. The floor you're on was the living room, and there are a couple of bedrooms above. I got some snowboarders staying in that one on the left up there. If they get too loud screwing, there's a broom in the closet that'll reach the ceiling." Gloria laughed at the look on Juno's face. "They look like the type, is all," Gloria went on, waving her paring knife in the air. "We were here until he was...well, ten or eleven, I'd say. Oh, he loved to sit on the stairs and listen to what was going on in the bar. Better than a television! Our regulars—we had some characters. Still do. That's Brattleboro. Small-town life, you know. It's different. Even when he was little, I knew it wouldn't be for him. You don't look like you've spent much time in a place like this."

"Maybe not exactly like this," Juno said thoughtfully, flicking the curl of potato skin from the knife.

"Small-town life wasn't for me either, though." She looked up at Gloria. "Especially not my small town. It's not the small part. It's the part that's yours. That's what made me leave, anyway." She picked another potato out of the crate. She was used to reading people, and it was a hard habit to turn off. But there was something about Monk's mother. Now she knew where he got it, the ability to move below her radar. His surface was as clear as the water she remembered from snorkeling on a rare vacation in Mexico once. The first spot was shallow, bright, full of yellow and blue fish that swam right up to her mask. Then they took a boat out far from the shore. The guide stopped in what seemed like the middle of nowhere, just a spot in the ocean, the boat dipping and tossing in choppy waves. Through darker water they dove, until Juno saw them, statues of people doing everyday things, reading the paper. Far below the surface, they carried out their mundane business in darkness, unobserved. Frozen in fascination and terror, Juno had forgotten to breathe and had to scramble to the surface, gasping. Sometimes in her dreams she'd find herself transformed into a statue at the bottom of the ocean, shuffling a deck of cards. Drinking coffee. Peeling potatoes.

"I imagine you might have some questions for me." Juno heard the words, astonished that they were hers and not Gloria's.

"Honey," Gloria said, placing the knife carefully on the cutting board. "I learned a long time ago not to ask a lot of questions. Like they say, curiosity kills."

"Only if you're a cat," Juno said, scraping the peeled potatoes into the pot.

"We're all cats here." Gloria started to stir with the big ladle. "Long-tailed cats. In a room full of rocking chairs." She put her hand on Juno's shoulder. "Sweetheart, go get me that big thing of cream—it's just inside, in the walk-in cooler back there."

Monk stepped into the cooler just as Juno found the cream. Juno couldn't help but notice how handsome he looked in an old fisherman's sweater and jeans. Like the calmer twin of the man she'd been with for the last few days. "I locked myself in here one time when I was a kid. Took them twenty minutes to figure out where I went."

"He had icicles in his hair." Gloria laughed. "I didn't think it was funny then, no sir. But he was always getting into someplace you never thought—remember the dumbwaiter?"

"Don't remind me. That was a nightmare."

"There used to be a dumbwaiter, over there. We boarded up after this guy decided to use it to sneak out of his room. And then one night—"

"I didn't calculate the fact that I was getting taller—"

"Oh no." Juno looked at the square of slightly different paint on the kitchen wall across the room.

"We could hear him, but his voice sounded like it was coming from everywhere and nowhere. Stuck between two floors in the damn dumbwaiter."

"Right. We had an Edgar Allan Poe situation."

"Well. I suppose it's my fault for naming you after one of his characters."

"Monk told me about that! You were a librarian?"

"Not exactly. I worked at the Brooks Library when I was in school. In a different life, I would have been a librarian. But we had the family business."

"The bar." Monk looked at his mother. She pursed her lips as if to whistle, but then she relaxed and smiled at Juno.

"Yes," she said, raising her eyebrows. "The bar. We all took care of the bar, and it was, you know, a full-time operation." Juno noticed Gloria looking back at Monk, who stood running a hand through his hair. His tell. "And then, you know. After Monk's father passed..."

"Ma, I thought I'd take Juno over to the Goose tonight. It's Tuesdays, still?"

"Oh, Monk. Don't. She doesn't want to sit around with that bunch of shriveled-up old men."

"Come on. You know she'd love Sal."

"Sal would love her! And then you'll have to rescue her. I see what you're up to."

"But first, the downtown tour. Get yourself dressed, Juno, and we'll get you that sweater you've been dreaming of."

"Wait, wait. You can't go back out in those sneakers you had on last night. There's more snow coming. What size do you wear? Take these boots; I bet we're close."

Juno put on the jeans and t-shirt she'd worn from

Vegas. Inside the closet, she found flannel shirts and wool sweaters, even a wool peacoat with a big floppy collar that hugged her shoulders perfectly. She carefully placed her trusty escape Keds in her bag where she always kept them before lacing on Gloria's hiking boots. The whole time she was dressing, she could hear their voices rising and falling everywhere and nowhere, like Monk and Gloria were trapped in the dumbwaiter. Monk, and then Gloria, and then Monk again. She couldn't hear the words, but she knew the sound of concerned discussion. Not fighting, because she knew well enough what that sounded like. Uncertainty. Sentences that ended with question marks.

Nineteen

"Ah, a local already." Monk met her at the bottom of the stairs and hugged her to him. Standing on the last step, she loomed an inch or two taller than him, and he turned his face up to hers with a goofy grin before burying his face inside the peacoat, between her breasts. "Mmm, you're warm," he mumbled. "Sorry; I'm freezing. I was just outside—"

Juno reached around his waist and thrust her hands into his back pockets, pulling his hips close to her to feel how hard he was, even through their layers of clothes. She leaned down slightly to kiss him violently, biting his icy-cold lower lip. Monk exhaled sharply and backed her up to the landing.

"You mother—"

"At her book club. It was a really long book this month. She'll be gone for hours."

"The bar—"

"Opens late on book club Tuesdays."

Monk unzipped her jeans; suddenly, the cold of his fingers inside her shot electricity up her spine. She cried out, and he covered her mouth with his as she balanced, her back against the wall and her hips tilted on the handrail. She felt one foot lift, and she draped her leg around his. She thought of his cold lips on her nipples and almost climaxed then and there. She started to pull up her sweater and shirt. Monk exhaled and enveloped one breast with his mouth while teasing the other nipple with his cold thumb, flicking and pressing it until it stood hard and pink. Then there it was, the shock and thrill of icy skin and the light pinch of teeth. She felt herself open completely as she called out his name.

She pushed Monk slightly, just enough to move him against the wall so she could lean into him as she unbuttoned his jeans, loosening his straining penis from inside. Monk moaned, spoke in garbled phrases, then shouted as she licked the shaft from the flat base of his balls all the way to the salty tip, slowly and without stopping. She flicked her tongue over the divot a few times, then let her mouth close around it and slide back down to the base again, pulling his balls down lightly with her hand. Monk shouted again, seemed to choke for a second, then inhaled long and loud. "Yes, oh, yes," he whispered as she moved her head up and down, his hands barely grazing her cheeks and hair at intervals. With one long "ahhh," he came; as he relaxed, Juno released her hold and her mouth suddenly, and Monk draped his body over her back, embracing her.

"Christ Almighty," he said.

"Good?" Juno asked brightly.

"I'm going to need a minute," Monk panted.

"There, there," Juno soothed, patting his leg. "Take your time. Oh, uh-oh."

"What?" Monk straightened a little. Juno laughed.

"It's that photo on the wall there. I didn't notice it before. That Civil War drummer boy."

"Yeah? That's Willie."

"He's looking right at us. Look. He does not approve. He's stopped drumming altogether. He's just staring."

"Willie's all right. He's just got a lot on his mind with the war and all."

That afternoon, they walked along the Connecticut River back to the bar, Monk carrying a small shopping bag full of warm new clothes for Juno and Juno carrying a box with a maple cake for Gloria.

"Over there on the other side, that's New Hampshire," Monk explained. "The Native Americans, the Abenaki, they called this place Wantastiquet."

Juno loved the sound of the word: hard and real, but with a mysterious beauty. "What does it mean? I mean, do you know what it means?"

"Some people say it means 'river to the west.' Some say 'lost river.' Or 'river of the lonely.' Evidently there is a word related to it the Abenaki used to describe a person who gives bad directions." Juno laughed. *That's how you know the truth*, her granny would say. *The truth won't be still for you.*

They stumbled out of the snow and into the orange light and laughter of the bar and its early evening regulars. As they passed the stairwell, Juno looked up and whispered, "You okay up there, Willie?"

"What up, Willie?" Monk muttered, waving to the photo. Gloria waved them over.

"I said I wouldn't believe it until I saw it with my own eyes! Look who's here!" An older man in a Carhartt jacket raised a pint of stout at Monk. Monk took off his knit hat, shook his hair free, and nodded while the bar patrons all called his name. "This is—" Monk began, but before he could finish, they all called out "Juno!" Juno waved and grinned.

"I made you some sandwiches to take. Eat some soup before you go; you know Sal never has any food but those damn beer nuts. That is, if you still insist on going."

"Where are we going?"

"Uncle Sal runs a poker game." Monk shrugged. "I don't know, you know, if you're at all interested in poker."

Juno threw back her head and laughed. "Oh, Monk. I'm dying for a table. You can see it on me, can't you? But your uncle..."

"Uncle Sal."

"Does your uncle Sal know what I do?"

"Not in so many words. Trust me. Sal's all right. I

feel like my job is to put the two of you at a table and get out of the way."

Juno squeezed Monk's hand. "Thank you," she said, "thank you, Monk." She kissed him, then hopped onto the bar stool.

Twenty

"Juno, that's what he does. Don't listen to him. Weren't you just complaining about your cards in the last hand? When you had three queens? He does this."

"What are you, a coach? We don't let coaches in here. She doesn't need a coach, anyway; she's killing me in here. Do you want to leave me a penniless old man?"

"Oh, please!" Monk waved his hands, while the men around the table grumbled. "Watch. He'll use his chip for more time now. Watch. This is what he does."

"What did I just say? Listen, it's none of my business, lady, but I don't think you need this guy."

"Are we playing or are we having a therapy session?"

"I'll raise to five hundred. Happy, Eddie?"

"I might be. Let's see the turn. Ah, fold, fold. I'm out."

Next to Eddie, another man threw in a handful of

chips. "I'll take some of that," said the next, tossing in his ante. Juno watched Sal's face while he narrated each move. "Abe, he's staying in. He's got nothing. He's got a dream. Tony's out. Shut up, Tony; you know you're out. You're holding a five and a six in your clammy hands like my sister's tits in the back row of the movie theater. Give up already." She had played hundreds of men with this kind of banter. All of Monk's distractions, his fakes and his tells, everything he'd pulled at the casino, she could see where he'd learned. The whole table was full of classic players. She could have taken these old boys to Vegas and cleaned out every tournament player on the circuit.

Tony was a master bluffer. He raised on principle, so you never knew whether he had the goods or not. Abe didn't speak at all, just peered over his glasses and under his shaggy eyebrows. Once in a while he'd hold up a finger as if calculating. Bennie feigned impatience, rattled his chips. And Sal monologued. He told dirty jokes and sex stories. He called out cards to see if he could get a blink out of a player. He spun long yarns that were hard to follow. "Sal, nobody even knows what you're talking about anymore," Angelo stacked his chips with a sigh, raising another five hundred.

"You betting on the river, Ang?"

"I think I just bet on the river, Sal. I forget a lot of things, but I think that's what I just did there." Eddie had folded on the turn. He sat with his arms folded across his chest, shaking his bald head.

"Look at him, he's so happy. Look at him checking

—Eddie, has he got a mirror under there? That's the only time Angelo looks so happy, when he's looking in a mirror."

"Quiet, please." Abe was holding his finger up in contemplation.

"Give me a break, professor. Abe's listening for the voice of Socrates." Sal began to intone, "Abraham, Abraham, the unexamined hand is not worth playing."

The grumbling around the table reached a crescendo as Abe folded. "Hey," Sal called out as Juno prepared to call. She had a pair of sevens, and the turn had yielded another. Three of a kind wasn't bad. It wasn't a hand to raise, but it wasn't a hand to fold. She had her hand on the chips. "Listen," Sal said, "if she wins this hand, I'll shut up for the next one."

Juno looked down at the table to avoid smiling. He knew she had something. Like Monk, Sal acted the clown, but he knew exactly where the table stood. He tracked it all while doing his act. Juno slid her chips across the table as the old men grumbled their approval. "Can I fold retroactively? I want her to win," Angelo said, pointing at Juno. Sal kept his dark eyes on her as he dropped two stacks of chips into the pot, calling. All the bets were in.

Angelo's two pair was a good hand, but not enough to beat Juno's three sevens. A cheer went up as she turned over her cards. "Not so fast, miscreants," Sal said, turning over his cards. "Full house, you jackals. Just to show you I'm good at heart, I'll only talk half as much for the next round." As he stacked the pile of chips in front of him, Sal began another promisingly lurid story. "Bennie, your brother-in-law's place, that warehouse? You know they found that body last week when they went to replace the furnace? They started jackhammering up the floor and— What?" Monk elbowed the old man, interrupting his train of thought, but not for long. "Anyway, you remember Pete? They said he went to California, but they're gonna find out something when they get those bones out." Monk put his head in his hands.

"Sal."

"What? It's Pete. We all knew it. Angelo knows. Bennie, your brother-in-law, he knows. We could save the forensics people some time and money. That's Pete in there."

"Maybe they'll find his wallet and they'll know."

Sal rolled his eyes. "Eddie, they're not going to find his wallet." More grumbles came from around the table. "Monk, I'm sorry. But you knew Pete wasn't in California."

Monk held up his hand. "Let's stop there, Sal," he said, irritated.

"Don't be sore at me now. You know Petey got in with the Russians and was bringing all kinds of... What, for Chrissakes?"

"Sal, can we not talk about this?"

"All of a sudden he's a fragile flower." Sal shrugged and tipped up the edges of his cards to check the new hands. "You been away, Monk."

"I've been away," Monk said, running both hands through his hair.

TWENTY-ONE

"I liked to think it was the river of the lost. Like it was the way to get to where you needed to be."

Monk stopped walking and held his gloved hand palm up. Juno took it. "We need to talk, don't you think?"

Monk nodded and turned back to the river, holding her hand tightly. "It's probably no surprise that I loved Peter Pan. The book, I mean. I've never seen any of the movies because, in my mind, the Lost Boys lived someplace down the Connecticut River on an island where Wendy read them books and they did magic tricks and acrobatics for her and no one was sad or missing. I didn't want to see it any other way." He paused and turned to Juno. "And no, there are no crocodiles in the Connecticut River. But to be honest, I was kind of surprised to find out crocodiles were real. I was ridiculously old when I saw one the first time."

Juno held his hand in both of hers. "Monk, you

don't appear to have a traditional job. But you have a private plane. You know everybody. You get calls and texts at all hours. At first, I thought you were a bookie."

Monk raised an eyebrow and nodded. "It's just..." he began, "we just...we don't, I mean we have never really talked about the family business."

"The family business? Isn't your family business a pub with an AirBnB?"

"Yeah. That's not the family business. I mean, it's a family business. It's the Davies family business."

"Your name isn't Davies?"

"No, it is. Legally and everything. I think we're starting in the middle, but that's just as well. Davies was my mother's maiden name. And the bar belonged to her father. She grew up in the bar. She would sit on the stairs and listen to the patrons. She got stuck in the dumbwaiter."

"She got stuck in the walk-in freezer."

"No, that one was legitimately my screw up. We moved and took over the bar when I was twelve. After my dad. After my dad was gone." Monk looked back out at the river. "We lived in New Jersey before that. I grew up in Jersey. Almost nobody knows. Mom came here right after Dad...and I've never gone back. Sal came with us. He's my father's brother. Sal Acosta. My father was Ray Acosta."

Juno stepped back. "Your father was Ray Acosta?" Even as far south as she had grown up, the stories had spread of Ray Acosta's disappearance. "But you're not..."

"I am. I'm Ray Acosta, Junior. Mom changed my name at first, thinking she could hide me away from all of it. But Sal found us. He told her if he could find us, then so could the rest of them. He told her it was better if she let him protect us. And he has. I'm sure they know who I am. But they've left me alone. They don't see me as a threat."

"And your business..."

"...is legitimate." Monk took Juno by the shoulders. "Let me be clear: my business is legitimate. Yes, I love to gamble. Yes, I still like the company of my uncle Sal, and he is a hazard. But I went to college, got a Masters in Finance, and I invested in land development, entertainment, and tech. So I know everybody in Vegas, yes. But trust me on this: I met Petey maybe once when I was about thirteen, and I have no idea how or why or even *if* Pete got himself interred in the foundations of Bennie's brother-in-law's warehouse."

"But Sal knows."

Monk stopped himself from running his hands through his hair. He shrugged instead. "Sal might know," he admitted.

"I should have known, really. I have an uncanny knack for finding the most dangerous man in the room." She kicked at a rock until it came loose. Then she picked it up and flung it as hard as she could into the lost river. When Monk first told her the translation, she hadn't imagined the Lost Boys at all. She'd imagined a river containing all the lost things, all down there in the river bed. Missing keys and wallets, lost dogs and cats, missing brothers and fathers. She watched the circles in the water and thought of Jack sitting down there, reading. Like she imagined him in the *Haunted House* pinball game. Like the statues under the sea in Mexico.

Monk was nodding. "Maybe so. Maybe I was the most dangerous man in the room. Because I followed a dangerous woman who cleaned my clock at the poker table. I followed her. At first because I wanted to follow trouble, and anybody back here in Brattleboro will tell you that is what I do. They did everything they could to keep me safe. But I thought my father was out there. I was afraid he couldn't find me with a new name." He stopped. "I'm sorry, Juno."

She stared at him through tears. "My name's not really Juno," she began, the words spilling out. "I mean, I did change it legally. But Mother named me Tammy. Juno was the name Jack called me to tease me. I was always reading things and saying 'd'you know this' or 'd'you know that,' so he started calling me Juno. After he was gone, I was afraid nobody would call me that and I'd never hear it again."

Juno started to sob, and Monk folded his arms around her. The river was high, the current dragging up limbs and trash in eddies and whirlpools. It smelled like more snow was coming.

"How can the world be big enough to swallow a person up," he whispered, "and small enough to make it impossible to hide?" He remembered thinking when Juno told him about Jack that he almost certainly must be dead. Standing on the banks of the river of wrong directions, Monk realized she knew Jack was out there the same way he knew his father was. Which was to say, possibly not at all, to any other person's eyes. He'd been looking everywhere. So had she. What they had found was each other.

"You and I," Juno said, "we know who we are. We named ourselves. We live on purpose. We found each other on purpose. I'm not afraid when I'm with you, not of anything."

Monk paused before kissing her, knowing that when he kissed this woman by the swirling waters of the loneliest river, he would never be able to forget her. He would never lose her to place, time, or memory. And then he kissed her, just before the streetlight came back on, long before the snow came and blotted out the sidewalks.

TWENTY-TWO

Juno charged down the stairs, stopping to pat Willie the Drummer Boy's face at the landing. There was a note on the bar that Monk had gone with Gloria to the produce market, something about a missing delivery. There was coffee and some fresh bread for toast, but Juno decided to pop back upstairs to get her boots and take a walk. She could probably make it to Gloria's favorite bakery and back before they were home from the market. She'd get herself a latte and surprise Gloria with her maple cake.

Seeing herself reflected in the shop windows, Juno thought back to that first morning in Vermont, Monk saying she looked like a local all bundled up. Her hair was soft and loose around her face; she hadn't combed it back into her usual severe style in weeks. She'd grown so fond of Gloria's hiking boots she hadn't worn her Keds once. She kept them safe and dry in her bag, because, as she had been taught never to forget, you never knew when you'd need to run.

She heard the barista's voice over the creaking of the shop's old wooden door. "Hey, Juno! Usual London Fog today?"

"Too early, Katie. I haven't had my coffee yet. Can I get a regular latte? And a maple cake if you have one ready."

"I'll wrap one up for you. Let me go get some more boxes. I'll be right back!"

Juno picked up one of the miniature log cabins on the counter and tried to peek into the window, half expecting to see a family of tiny bears inside. A month ago, she'd have claimed this whole cozy cottage vibe did not appeal to her in the slightest. But the last few weeks of cards with Uncle Sal, backgammon and Patriots games with the regulars in the bar, and of course the nights with Monk—and the mornings, and the afternoons—she had found a rhythm. It felt right. *This is what people do*, she thought. She smiled and wondered if Monk was thinking the same thing. He hadn't once mentioned Vegas.

She first saw him reflected in the mirrored bakery case. So she thought she was daydreaming, having a walking nightmare. She would do that sometimes. In moments of great happiness, her worst fears would seem to manifest. *I have to stop doing this to myself*, she thought. *I deserve to be happy*. She turned around and no one was there.

"Katie," Juno called. "I'm going down to the grocery, but I'll be right back for the cake."

The door creaked again as she exited to the street. The sidewalk was mostly clear each way, except for Mr. Thompson and his beagle waiting to cross at the corner. Juno crossed in the middle of the block and turned left, back toward the bar. Mr. Thompson was coming toward her.

"Hey, Fritter!" Juno greeted the dog and bent down to scritch his ears. "How's your day going, Mr. Thompson?"

"Very well, Miss Juno. Fritter and I have finished our errands and will be having lunch in the park."

"Oooh, that sounds lovely, but cold! Will you be warm enough?"

"I have Fritter's coat in my pocket and soup in my thermos. We won't stay too long. Will we see you for backgammon tonight?"

"You bet!" *Everything is fine*, she thought. She petted Fritter once more and then watched them walk down the block toward the park. When they turned the corner, she turned around.

He was standing right in front of her. It really was Mitchell. He had found her.

Twenty-Three

She couldn't even remember agreeing to go with him to the diner outside town. She sat in the booth furious with herself for getting into a car with him, a car! She remembered her mother watching episode after episode of *20/20*, saying, "Baby, if they ever get hold of you, you fight like hell. Don't let 'em take you to crime scene number two. That's where they gone kill you."

It wasn't crime scene number two. It was a tourist diner full of snowboarders eating waffles. But she'd failed on a crucial point. Sitting there in the booth, she decided it would be the last time she'd give in to Mitchell without a fight.

She had ordered coffee. Mitchell was carefully cutting an egg white omelet into small pieces, looking up at her occasionally. He took one bite and stopped as if considering the entire situation for the first time.

"Finding you was difficult. Time-consuming." He

chewed and talked. "I've had to delay meetings and inconvenience important people."

Juno knew what he was doing. Tearing her down. Making her feel like she had made trouble, that she had misbehaved.

"So sorry," she said, sipping her coffee, "that your important people were inconvenienced."

"I see. You have interpreted what I said to mean something I did not intend at all. You think I meant to imply that you are not important. Quite the contrary. I've stopped everything in my life to find you and keep you safe. You underestimate the level of risk in which you've placed yourself."

Mitchell's second level of attack: veiled threats. There's risk, all right. But he's not her protector. Juno knew what protection felt like, and this was not it.

"I'm aware of the threat," she said, crossing her arms and meeting his gaze. Mitchell looked away, as if searching for the napkin that was in his lap.

"Well." Mitchell dabbed his lips with the napkin. Juno shuddered to remember a time when she ached to kiss those lips. In the early days of their romance, Mitchell was just as eager. Back when she was still playing tournaments, Mitchell flew to the Bahamas to meet her. He was waiting for her in the bar when she came out of the casino. In the elevator on the way to the room, he had kissed her neck, her mouth, her eyelids. Barely inside their suite, he pulled her to the marble entry floor, pushed her dress up, and pressed his face between her legs. His tongue fluttered inside her until she couldn't breathe. The climax was so acute she hadn't been able to stand his touch for minutes after.

In those early days, Mitchell slept in the same bed with her all night. They would read and make love in the mornings. After a few weeks, Mitchell would wait for her to fall asleep and then either go back to work or to sleep in his own bedroom. Juno had never slept in Mitchell's room. He called it his office, but it was a suite with its own sleeping area. She'd only been inside it once or twice. The last time she saw Mitchell's penis, oddly enough, was in his office.

It was late at night. She'd woken up alone, which wasn't unusual. At the time, Juno still felt inextricably drawn to Mitchell. His withholding, his preference for oral sex only, his absence from her bed—all of it, she realized now, had created a gnawing need for his attention in her. She had crept through the door to his office and found him sitting in front of a wall of monitors.

He had pretended not to see her at first. When she touched his shoulder, he looked up at her without surprise and without joy. Juno mistook his emptiness for sadness. She slipped onto his lap, grinding against him until he became partially erect. When Juno began to edge down to her knees to take him into her mouth, he pushed her back onto the floor. "Please," Juno had begged him. Sitting there in the booth three years later, Juno found it dizzying and disgusting that she had longed for him so terribly. Among the exuberant snowboarders, their bright hats and scarves, their waffles and strawberries, Juno felt the shame at the edges of her heart.

"I understand," Mitchell said, reaching into his pocket, "this isn't really the romantic gesture I could have planned and I'm sure you would have preferred."

Feigned deference. Juno swallowed more coffee. Mitchell placed a small black box on the Formica table, careful to center it as exactly as possible while avoiding a sticky patch of syrup.

"Please open it. It's a special metal, Palladium. An American version of platinum. I thought you'd prefer it. I know your aversion to diamonds."

Juno stared at the black box like it was a bomb.

"Mitchell, it won't work. I won't marry you."

"No, you will. We will be married at the house or at the apartment in town. It's arranged. And then, a perpetual honeymoon. You can have anything you like. We can travel. And I can assure you, you won't leave my sight again."

Juno stood up and walked toward the restaurant exit. She didn't look to see if Mitchell followed or not. In the parking lot, his suits caught her by the arms. Nothing forceful enough to make a scene, and Juno had completely expected to be delayed. She had been rehearsing exactly what she was going to say.

Twenty-Four

"Mitchell. You don't want to do this."

Mitchell cocked his head to the side like a crow. "No, you're mistaken. I very much want to do this. You know that better than anyone. I only do the things I want to do."

"I don't want to do this, Mitchell. I don't want to marry you. Are you saying that I have to do things I don't want to do, and you don't? That's not much of a partnership."

Mitchell looked at the black box in his hand with an expression of consternation. Then he looked back at Juno and smiled. "That's not right, though. Not exactly. You're emotional, and that prevents you from making clear decisions. But I'm confident it will pass. Right now, you can't understand why this option is the right one for us. We have a history, and that history is very, very important to me. As it should be to you, because that's what's keeping you alive. You left, without a word. I'm sure I've done some things that might have triggered you to make that decision...and that I apologize for."

"Don't be condescending to me, Mitchell." *Did he really think I was buying this line of bullshit?* she thought to herself. *He'd never apologized to anyone a day in his life, nor did she believe he meant a word of it. Why would he change now?*

"Now, Juno." Mitchell's face turned grave. "I had hoped to avoid all of this. But if you insist, I will help you to understand why us being together is best for everyone."

"We're in a public parking lot. I've established myself in this town. If I am missing, it will be noticed. People will care that I'm gone." Juno's voice cracked slightly. Only as she said the words out loud did Juno realize the change that had happened. Someone would notice. People would notice if she disappeared. It would matter. Katie would wonder why she hadn't picked up her cake. Mr. Thompson would have to play backgammon with someone else. Gloria would have to chop the vegetables for soup and water the plants. Sal would have to make up new stories instead of retelling the ones all the boys at the table had already heard.

And Monk. Her eyes stung, but she stood straight and fixed her eyes on Mitchell, who looked everywhere else but at Juno. "I think you misunderstand. I only want you to leave with me if it's what you want. I agree it has to be mutual beneficial, this partnership."

"Then we have nothing to talk about."

"All I ask is that you hear me out before you make a final decision. I have a meeting in New York, so I will be leaving here..." Mitchell stretched his arm grandly to examine his watch. "I will be leaving in twelve minutes at the most."

"I don't need twelve minutes to tell you 'no' again."

"Listen, Juno. Just listen. And think. I know you don't want to hear it right now, but I do love you. I always have. I might not be offering you the most traditional life, but that's not who you are." Mitchell surveyed the parking lot, the minivans full of families and teenagers suited up for a day in the snow. "Come on. You're telling me this is your kind of place? I know you better than that." He chuckled and stuffed his hands deep into the pockets of his cashmere coat. "Marry me, Juno. Marry me tomorrow in the city. The real city. I've taken care of everything; you don't have to lift a finger. From then on, it's whatever you want. Since you will be my wife, you will be provided with a monthly allowance, of course. And you'll have a dedicated spot on the XK3 shuttle one day, too."

Juno burst out laughing. "Do I also get a set of steak knives? Really, Mitchell—"

He stepped closer, almost touching her face with his extended finger. "That's twice you have interrupted me. I am still speaking." His face reddened, but then he collected himself. "Also, I will help you find your brother Jack."

Juno had never even told Mitchell about Jack. An

emotion welled inside her that felt like anger, outrage. She'd put away the dream of Jack like an old diary, and it was as if Mitchell were standing in front of her tearing out the pages. She must have moved, because she felt the bodyguard's hand on her arm. She squared her shoulders and freed herself. *I'm going to enjoy refusing him this one last time,* she thought.

Mitchell looked again at his watch, disapprovingly.

"Very well. Here is the second option. You can decide if this future is one you could see yourself in. Staying here in this...place..."

He doesn't even know where we are, Juno thought. But she listened. He was angry now. She had embarrassed him, and even she knew that was not a good situation to be in.

"You can stay here and live here, do as you like. Within one month, there will be an announcement that the XK3 Nuclear Waste Remediation Research Facility will break ground one mile upriver from this adorable town. There will be a legal objection that will stall the project initially, but a circuit court judge, and old friend of mine with some interesting and unusual habits and preferences, will overturn the injunction, and we will install the largest nuclear waste facility the world has ever seen right here. In two weeks, Sal Acosta will be arrested and indicted for murder and racketeering. Never met the man in person, but in the early days of my business education, shall we say, I crossed paths with some of his associates. He's not well-liked in many circles, that cute little man. You'd be surprised.

Anyway, he will be convicted in a Federal court in a bench trial, and he will spend the rest of his life in jail. Which will, somewhat fortunately for all concerned, not be a very long time. In one week," Mitchell went on, as calmly as if he were discussing his meeting schedule, "the entire block on which Davies Tavern is situated will be purchased by a development consortium. Everything will be bulldozed to the ground, including the Brooks Library."

He paused, watching her. She knew it wasn't over. She steadied herself.

"In two days, Monk Mason Davies will disappear. No one will investigate."

Juno stood frozen, resolute at least not to show Mitchell he had hit the mark. She had no choice. He saw the recognition in her eyes.

"'Just like his father,'" Mitchell said slowly. "That's what everyone will say."

Mitchell had several conditions for Juno, the first of which was the surrender of her phone. She would not return to Brattleboro at all. There was no need. There had been an interval of significance, Mitchell explained, but not a protracted one, and everyone was sure to go right on with their lives without delay.

Juno had one condition. She asked for a wedding in Istanbul, professing a childhood love for Byzantine architecture. She had dreamed of visiting the Hagia Sophia since reading about it in the school encyclopedia and seeing the glossy photos of its miraculous dome.

Mitchell remained silent for a few minutes, considering the request as part of the negotiation. "Fine," he said at last. "Glad to see you've come around. You and I will be very happy together."

Mitchell seemed calmer and very satisfied with himself as he excused himself to the back seat of the SUV, closing the partition as he explained the series of emails he needed to write on the way back to New York. Juno felt it was a small mercy to be rid of him for a couple of hours at least. She curled up against the door. She didn't test it. She knew it would be locked. From now on, all the doors would be locked. She felt inside her bag for her running away shoes. They'd be ready when she had her chance. Mitchell could lock the doors. He could threaten and bully. But Mitchell had no idea how vast his underestimation of her would turn out to be.

Juno leaned her head on the cold window of the SUV, watching the Connecticut River, the lost river, roil and spill. She dreamed of herself at the bottom, shuffling a deck of cards.

Twenty-Five

The inky black of the Atlantic at night stretched below. Once in a while she saw lights on the horizon, a ship of some kind, too far for her to signal in distress. And it wouldn't do her any good. She wasn't ready to surrender yet.

Juno couldn't help remembering her last trip in the co-pilot's seat. A very different trip that was. Mitchell's man wasn't nearly as friendly as Pilot Alan. He just sat there wearing an indifferent expression, even when she asked how far the Bermuda Triangle might be and whether he might could just fly them directly into it. So she had wrapped herself in an XK3Space fleece blanket and settled back, watching for signs of life in the darkness.

On the edge of sleep, she heard the cockpit door crack open. The pilot stood as Mitchell slid into the seat and took the controls. Juno pretended to doze, and for a long time Mitchell kept silent.

"We could have a great life, you know. Plenty of women would be more than satisfied with the kind of world I can make for you, Juno. I missed you. It wasn't the same without you."

Juno hardly moved, but she rolled her eyes behind her closed lids.

It was all she could do to keep quiet. But Juno knew the speech too well. He wasn't done. Pretty soon he'd get tired of complimenting her, and he'd start telling her how the problem was her. That if she weren't so selfish, they could be happy together. Instead, Mitchell stopped, and it was quiet for some minutes except for the rumble of the jet engines. Then they stopped. Juno opened her eyes but kept her back to Mitchell, waiting. They did not seem to be losing altitude. But it was too dark to say for certain. Juno scanned for a light point on the horizon, but nothing appeared.

"Don't worry," Mitchell said softly, as if talking to a child. "We haven't run out of fuel. I've turned off the engines."

Not especially consoling, Juno thought. But she didn't move. He went on as if he knew she was listening, but she gave no indication.

"We could glide for quite a few minutes this way. If we had run out of fuel, we'd be okay over land. I'd look for a flat space, a field, something clear of power lines and population."

Juno thought about how she would press her face against the window next to her bed at night after the trailer park lights had gone out. It would be too dark to see anything but her own hazy reflection. Here she was again, flung out into the universe protected only by a flimsy metal tube, with no idea what was about to happen next. She had been more afraid as a little girl. Afraid she'd be erased like Jack. Except he wasn't erased. He was out there. More importantly, he was in here with her. In the plane, in her heart. And she would not be erased, either. She was part of the river that always came back, the last round of the hand when the secrets came out. The place where all the lost would be found.

"I could turn them back on. I have time." Juno wondered what Mitchell would want in exchange for saving them.

"Most people don't know that commercial planes turn off their engines sometimes for minutes at a time while pilots have dinner or take bathroom breaks. But if you leave them off too long, you pass the point of rescue. If you test the boundaries for too long, you can find yourself unreachable."

Just crash the plane, Juno thought, *with as little conversation as you can manage.*

As if he could hear her thoughts, Mitchell went silent. After what seemed like hours, Juno heard the engines purr back to life.

"I could have sent us into the Atlantic," Michell said simply. This time it sounded more like he was talking to himself. "Not this time, though. Not yet."

She turned and stretched. "How much longer

until we land in Istanbul?" she asked, stifling an authentic yawn.

TWENTY-SIX

J uno picked Istanbul for several reasons, the first of which was that she knew the airport where they would have to land. Despite his power and influence, there would be no private airports this trip for Mitchell. It was harder to circumvent local authority in Turkey; the country took smuggling of goods and information equally seriously. Even though Mitchell would have to land at Istanbul Airport, a bustling, sprawling facility, he would have access to private screening and expedited customs processing. She would not have a lot of time.

But she had a plan. Juno stepped in front of Mitchell, taking off her shoes and placing her bag on the inspection table. "Can you clear me first? I need to visit the ladies' room." An official in a blue cap was already checking Mitchell's pockets while Mitchell unlocked his laptop and cell phone. Instead of stopping, the official in the blue cap gestured to two other men in gray caps. They came and emptied Juno's bag, taking a few moments to inspect her wallet and lipstick. One of them placed her running-away shoes over his white gloved hands, marching them across the table. He smiled at Juno, and she laughed. With great care, they returned her few items to the bag and handed it back to her. Juno put her shoes back on but left her bag on the inspection table. She knew how Mitchell thought. What, she was going to disappear into the Istanbul Airport with no bag, no money, no phone, no passport? He wouldn't think twice. As long as she was back quickly.

She left the Customs Office and walked slowly until she found a restroom farther down the International Concourse. Ducking into the first stall, she pulled off her left running-away shoe and ripped out the insole. She was pretty sure the CCTV cameras did not record the activity within the bathroom stalls themselves, but at this point, she didn't care. By the time anyone Mitchell knew might wonder why Juno was taking apart her shoe in the bathroom in the Istanbul Airport, the information would be out in the world. The shell companies, the money Mitchell claimed to donate to charitable organizations, all of which he had set up to launder and funnel money right back to his own accounts. For years, Mitchell had been defrauding the government with massive tax deductions. Never mind the fraud he had committed against scores of donors. All of it was fake. The only charity Mitchell really funded was himself.

Mitchell knew she had found out. But he didn't know that she had long ago crept into his bedroom during one of his space training weekends. He didn't know she had figured out the code to bypass the fingerprint scanner by watching the cleaning staff. He certainly didn't know she had used a simple thumb drive to copy enough of his personal financial records to prove he was depositing the money from his charitable organizations into a series of accounts in the Cayman Islands. She wondered what the inevitable interviews would be like. Mitchell sincerely believed he deserved that money, that his contribution to history would be much greater than most people's simple minds could fathom.

All this time, Juno's running away shoes weren't just a way to move more quickly than she could manage in high heels. Carved into the footbed of the left shoe, tucked under the insole she had glued back in place, was a space just long and wide enough for a thumb drive. One that had avoided airport security as long as it probably could, she thought. The fear of getting caught with the thumb drive wasn't her main reason for acting now. *But it's definitely an incentive,* Juno thought, laughing. She wasn't sure what it would mean for her, Mitchell's coming reckoning. But she knew what doing nothing would mean, and she couldn't live with that option. At least she hadn't married him yet. Maybe she wouldn't go to jail.

Juno curled her fingers around the thumb drive she had retrieved from her shoe. She kept it hidden in her palm and left the stall. Now came the moment when she would have to use every skill she'd honed at the poker table, every nuance and gesture she'd learned to read. She tucked the thumb drive in her sleeve and washed her hands, studying in the mirror the line of women behind her waiting for stalls. A Lufthansa attendant who looked pale, possibly sick or dehydrated, shifting uncomfortably. Two dark-haired teenagers playing a game on their phones, their heads bent and almost touching, laughing and gently nudging each other. A British Airways flight attendant in her mid-thirties, an older American woman dressed in a gray Eileen Fisher pantsuit and Prada sneakers, another teenaged girl with a travel pillow around her neck.

Juno chose the British Airways flight attendant. She met her eyes first as she walked toward her, smiling as if recognizing her. "Hey," she said brightly, and the attendant smiled, knitting her eyebrows in curiosity. She took Juno's hand when she extended it. "Take this." The attendant's eyes widened slightly. Juno felt the woman's fingers find and secure the thumb drive. She only nodded, and Juno never stopped, kept walking through the passageway, back out into the International Concourse.

As she emerged from the restroom archway, two men with headsets flanked her and kept pace until she approached the glass doors to the private Customs Office. She could see Mitchell standing next to the table with his hands clasped in front of him. He must have sent the pilot ahead with their bags. The men stepped in front of Juno and blocked her from entering.

"I'm sorry, Miss, but you will have to come with us. We are holding your fiancé for questioning."

Well, that was fast, Juno thought. But she smiled at the agents and offered her arm.

TWENTY-SEVEN

Mitchell had been held for questioning for long enough that Juno couldn't be sure they hadn't taken him to a police station, or worse. The men who had followed her in the concourse had retrieved her bag for her before taking her to a waiting room like something in a spa. She'd poured herself a tall glass of water fragrant with citrus, stretched out on a tufted divan, and slept soundly for the first time in days. Her keepers asked her only one question: would there be anything that would make the lady more comfortable? *Raki*, yes? Juno smiled and shook her head. She knew alcohol consumption came with a host of complications in Turkey. The Islamist government disapproved, but *raki* was part of Turkey's cultural legacy. Still, best not to chance it. Not knowing much about her situation, she steered clear of any choices at all and went quickly to sleep.

She didn't think of herself as a believer in the

supernatural. If there were forces in the universe beyond her, they certainly hadn't often reached out with any messages or answers to her prayers. But in her sleep, Juno traveled. She retraced her flight over the ocean, her drive through New York and up along the coast until she reached the snow. Until she found the river. She went down to the river of the lost people and waded into it. Once she was up to her knees, she stopped. "It's not time," she whispered.

She floated up Main Street past the post office and the library. It was dusk, or maybe early morning, but no one was out and the postal trucks sat in their row covered in snow. She saw lights on in the bar, but she didn't go in the front door. She didn't run her hand along the rail or say hello to Willie the drummer on the landing. She floated to the upstairs window and saw him inside, asleep under the quilts. She tried to put a hand on the windowpane, and suddenly she was in the warm room, the smells of cedar and cinnamon and whiskey enveloping her. She crawled under the covers and found Monk, his skin burning, his lips soft. He moaned in his sleep and pulled her close. She kissed his neck, his chest, the line of soft brown hair down his belly to his cock, already hard. She slid her entire body along his until she sat on top of him, taking him inside her all at once. Monk called her name and sat up, but he did not open his eyes. He grasped her hips; she pulled his face to her breast and stroked his hair as she rocked back and forth.

Juno woke up several hours later with little sense of

how long she had been in the room with the two guards. They had covered her with a light cotton blanket, tightly knit with blue stripes and fringe. She didn't move at first, just listened to the guards and their soft conversation. She only understood the words occasionally, but the casual tone and inflection caused her no alarm. When they saw her eyes were open, they smiled and nodded to her, then continued talking to each other. She thought of reaching for her bag, but there was nothing to tell her anything there. No phone, no watch. She sat up slowly and stretched, surveying the room. No clock. Like a casino. She laughed, and the guards stopped to look at her. *They must think I'm an idiot. Or crazy.* Juno decided either option was a perfectly fine way for the guards to think of her. Then she did reach for her bag, slowly. She sat cross-legged on the divan and placed the bag in her lap, drawing out all the cosmetics she had with her, along with her small hairbrush. The guards settled back into conversation as she applied lipstick, highlighter, and brow gel. They regarded her with some interest as she took the clips out of her choppy hair, brushed, and rearranged it. She took out a scarf she had bought in the airport and tied it so as to cover her hair. *Modesty is never controversial*, she thought.

Once she finished, she reclined again, trying to sleep or at least refocus her thoughts. No strategy presented itself. Juno never knew what to do in such cases. Her life had always depended on anticipating the next move. She'd spent a lot of time in windowless rooms with no clocks. Even when those rooms had men with guns at the door. But usually she'd be looking at a few particular cards and calculating whether or not the deck would fall in her favor. Assessing which people in the room might be desperate enough to reveal themselves and their triumphs or failures. Watching each player for a sign of hope or betrayal.

In this room, there was nothing to watch but two innocuous-enough guards who seemed to be interested in getting home in time for a soccer match. If she were playing these guys, she'd bluff them and they'd fold easily. With what cards? If she had cards right now, what would they be? And what round? She had assumed, since she really didn't have any idea what was happening, this was the pre-flop. Barely any way to know what anyone held, only the first round of betting to go on. No community cards. Nobody knew where they were.

But what if it's not? What if she'd already seen one or two streets of play and it was actually the Turn? What if Mitchell's arrest was the fourth card turned up? She knew this whole scenario had nothing to do with the thumb drive full of damning tax evasion evidence. That flight attendant was probably on the way to Lisbon or Marseille, or maybe Cairo—it could take hours or even days for her to take any action. She'd go back and tell her friends, her supervisor, maybe the pilot if she trusted him. Because Juno knew, as some people know, that airlines have code names in order to alert staff to suspected domestic abuse while they are in flight. The last thing you wanted to do halfway over the Atlantic Ocean was alarm an abusive partner. Juno read faces. When she handed her the thumb drive, she knew she'd hit the mark when she saw the woman's facial muscles tense and her pupils dilate.

So what were the community cards, the facts anyone could see? Mitchell, a rich, famous American inventor and influencer whose money and influence seem to dissolve any barrier. His money, his business. What was his profile? Space. Technology. Information. Juno sat up a little and put her feet on the floor. She'd changed into her running-away shoes. Maybe they were actually running toward something. If it was in fact the Turn, only one thing could be next: the River.

TWENTY-EIGHT

Juno thought she might have to clamp her hand over her mouth to stifle the laughter that kept bubbling up as they rode to their villa on the eastern peninsula. Mitchell continued to seethe, his leg popping up and down as it always did when he was especially vexed. Since becoming XK3 over a decade ago, Mitchell had completely forgotten what it was like to be told "no." Being detained by Turkish police must have seemed to him like being abducted by aliens.

The villa overlooked the Riva where it joined the Black Sea. In the distance, Juno could see the Riva Kalesi, the castle that had survived from the Byzantine era. According to the Greeks, Jason stopped there looking for the Golden Fleece. He didn't find what he wanted here, either.

Juno did her best to avoid Mitchell. His mood had gone from frantic to black. For the first few days, Mitchell had continued to plan their wedding, even asking Juno her opinion on certain matters. The dinner menu, the floral display. No guests were invited. He said there were no need for vows to be exchanged. Contractual aspects would be handled separately, of course. For the ceremony itself, Mitchell had hired a local composer who was bringing a small string quartet who would play as they exchanged rings.

"And you will receive your microchip as well," Mitchell explained to her. Juno nodded. Of course. She thought about the stray cat she'd kept a few days, long enough to start calling it a name other than "cat" or "hey you." It turned out to belong to a family that lived two streets over, according to the shelter. They had little kids. The cat's real name was Mickey. She'd called him Frank, which she liked a lot better, and she figured the cat did, too. Who named a cat after a mouse? But she gave him back. They were little kids.

"Microchip?" This time, she had to ask. Typical Mitchell, his world revolved around his latest and greatest techno gadgets. Was that even legal? To put a chip in someone? The cat had a chip; that's how the shelter knew what family it belonged to. Apparently, she was now being treated like a cat. Only she belonged to Mitchell, which was much worse.

"Of course." Mitchell's mouth twitched, almost into a smile. He tried to force open the gap in her silence. "It will contain your health information, and it will open all the facility doors throughout XK3 Land and XK3 Space."

"No need for keys," Juno said brightly. *They'll open*

exactly the doors you want me to open and none of the others, she thought to herself.

"Exactly! And of course, I will always be able to locate you in case anything ever happens. Give or take a few feet. There's a lot of dangerous people out there who wouldn't mind a hefty ransom. And I don't want to have to worry about these people taking advantage of you being my wife." *Yes*, she thought. *He admitted the real reason. A chip in my arm so he can track me. Well, what difference does it make? He found me without a chip. It's beside the point. There's only one way I'm ever getting out from under him, and it's going to take some time.*

Mitchell had also flown in a dress maker from Italy to create a wedding dress for Juno. The fabric was flown in as well, Italian silk, and it was beautiful. The lace was sourced locally by a local dress maker. The design was a simple and elegant combination, probably for practical purposes. Juno remembered a small photo of Mitchell's mother in her wedding gown in his apartment, and she couldn't help but think there was a part of him wanting to see that dress recreated on her. She wondered what he would have been like if she was still around; whenever he talked about her, he would soften a little. It made him seem human.

Juno opened the French doors to her bedroom, not caring if the security alarms went off. She stepped out onto the vast balcony with its expanse of mosaic tile and walked all the way to the corner. The Greeks believed the Black Sea hated strangers. From further

North came stories about a man with an arrow for an arm, one that could boil water, melt earth, and set the air on fire. She wasn't superstitious, but the old stories she read in the school library sometimes predicted the future in ways that frightened her. An arrow that could set the world on fire. They must have seen these days coming in the roiling Black Sea, its strangely turbulent waters. So they made up a story about the end of the world, a story that ended with the arrow at the bottom of the ocean.

She thought carefully about where she was standing. Not just over the violent Black Sea rocking and breaking over the arrow of destruction, but where she stood in the game Mitchell did not even know he was playing. Only the Flop cards were face up. The River was still coming. She stood on the balcony and pretended to be an Argonaut rowing across the Black Sea under the command of a crazy egotist on a ridiculous mission. She imagined herself an archer in the army of the caliphate, marching into battle against the mercenaries hired by the Byzantines to protect Constantinople, the capitol they were doomed to lose. She'd sat at enough tables to trust the feeling rising along her skin. The card coming was hers.

TWENTY-NINE

"Juno, I'm offering you a chance to be my partner in life. You know my life is my business, and it's true the other way around, too. I'm not going to pretend with you. You're too smart for that. You know part of this marriage is my insurance policy, my guarantee of your loyalty. But I'm hoping you'll become part of the forward-facing arm of the operation. Think about it. My beautiful, brilliant wife. You do anything you want, sell clothes, throw parties, whatever." Juno winced. He didn't seem to know her at all.

"I'm not a monster. You'd see that if you'd just think about it. I love you. I've always loved you. Everything I've done is for you."

Mitchell walked over to her. He held her face in both his hands, the first affectionate gesture he'd offered her in weeks. *He still knows how to get to me,* she thought. She tried not to look into his eyes, tried not to remember anything good in him. He might be offering her a life of money and power, but it would be a life of obligation. And fear. Once she was his wife, if Mitchell's shady deals came to light, she could go to jail right beside him.

"Let me do something special for you. Let's find Jack. Together."

Mitchell overplayed the hand. Juno shook free, then stared back at him. Anything old light in his eyes was gone for her. She searched in them now for a tell, something to show her if Mitchell already knew where Jack was, if he was keeping him so he could play the hero with her. It was a crazy thought, she knew. Jack disappeared when she was a kid. Mitchell would have been a teenager, still coding games in his parents' garage.

But what if he'd already used his influence and connections? What if her own attempt to find Jack had come up short because Mitchell had found him already? She'd followed Jack's path into Canada, but from there, his trail went cold. For the last year, she'd been stuck. Maybe there was a reason she wasn't just five steps behind now. Maybe there was a really good reason the steps had stopped altogether.

"Where is he, you bastard!" She grabbed at Mitchell's jacket, her hand sliding off the lapel. She caught wherever she could, flailing at Mitchell. She wasn't sure if she was trying to hurt him or shake the truth out of him. Mitchell turned suddenly, and the jacket tore along the seam of his pocket, which was still in her fierce grip.

Mitchell backed away, straightening his collar and smoothing his hair. "Tell you what," he said, clearing his throat. "I'm going to leave you alone for a bit. You should think about spending this time in search of your sense of gratitude. I'll be back in a few days."

Juno felt something like electricity along her spine. She didn't know it yet, but the River card had just been dealt.

Thirty

Juno walked the halls of the villa, feeling calm in Mitchell's absence. But as the days passed, she worried. She didn't particularly care what happened to him, she told herself. She'd already made that decision when she sent his financial records out into the world like a message in a bottle.

Juno started exploring the other floors of the villa. She wandered into a topiary maze, finding statues and benches to rest on inside before she made her way across. On the other side, she found the guesthouse whose roof she'd seen from the edge of the balcony.

She walked toward the door on the path but then went around the side, hidden in the Judas trees she recognized from the paintings on the walls of the Hagia Sophia. She looked through a window to find the room empty. Through the glass, she saw the computer screen on the desk, open to an email.

The door to the guesthouse had a lock pad, but it

opened easily without so much as a beep. That email began, "The Feds are in Miami and Los Angeles. They've taken all the computers and boxed up any paper they could find. What do you want us to do?" She rifled through the mostly empty desk drawers, not even sure what she was trying to find. She took some papers from the printer, shocked that Mitchell allowed anyone in his organization to print anything. *Was he gone?* she wondered as she started to feel anxious and excited at the thought of it being that easy. But then she started thinking, really thinking, about how she was going to get out. She wanted to explain as little as possible on the way out of Turkey. Mitchell still hadn't told her why he had been detained, and she'd had no access to a phone or even a person who might shed some light on what had happened at the airport. So she dropped the papers back into the tray and moved on.

Technology. Juno suspected it was Mitchell's connection to technology and information that had run him into trouble with the Turkish authorities. It had to be. Maybe she could find something in the scraps left behind here. But what did it matter, anyway? Whatever got Mitchell out of her life. Juno had seen this situation before. A player holding the nuts on a big hand, the pot out of control, and something unexpected happened. Somebody weaved a web, and damn if it didn't catch. Even a veteran player could forget the math under the spell of a good yarn. He knew he's going to win, but in the story, he lost. He came to believe the story. Then the story came true: he folded, it's all a bluff, but it's too late. He'd lost.

She had also seen the opposite happen. It had happened enough to her. She'd have nothing, maybe a low pair, and she'd know who had the aces. But that electricity along her spine would kick in, and she would know: *I win. In my story, I win this hand.* And she would start to tell the story in which she won.

Mitchell made the bet. Mitchell had the cards in his hand. The river card lay open for the showdown. There was nothing left but nerve, Juno's nerve. And it was rock solid.

In the guest house bedroom, Juno saw the safe hanging open. If she hadn't realized it before, she now knew they had cleared out in a hurry just before her discovery. Hardly anything of use remained. But in the very back of the safe, a couple of burner phones lay tucked in a corner.

Juno's hands shook as she dialed the international code. *Cell phones*, she thought, *have made it a lot harder to remember phone numbers.* But the phone rang twice before she heard a man's voice.

"I need help," she said, her words catching in her throat.

THIRTY-ONE

"You're lucky I picked up, lady," the voice crackled out. "I thought you were the FBI, and I was going to give you hell. Perks up my afternoon sometimes."

"Well, if you're bored, I've got something even more fun than messing with the FBI."

"Shut your mouth. There's no such thing." Juno heard something muffled, and then he was back. "You got me, girlie. Tell Uncle Sal every little thing you need."

Back in Brattleboro, Juno played poker with Sal and his friends every Tuesday. Sometimes Monk would come along, but he never played. "They raised me," Monk would say. "When I play them, I play them like I'm nine years old and they just taught me how last week. I can't bluff, and they sucker me for fun. No thanks. You give it a try. That's my revenge. Take their money, please."

Poker on Tuesday nights, then Juno started coming to Sal's tidy brick ranch house in the afternoons to watch old *Law & Order* episodes. "Not that SUV one," Sal would say. "I like the cute broad, that Hargitay girl. I knew Mickey, did I tell you? Anyway, I don't watch that one. Not the kids. I don't want to see kids hurt."

Sal had roses, but they were dormant for winter. "You come back in the spring," he told Juno, "and I'll make you a collar big enough for Secretariat. You like red, pink, white? I got peach, yellow. I got this one that's lavender, almost gray. Had to ship it in. The florist doesn't have that one. You come see."

Sal would make them amaretto coffee to drink with hard anise cookies while he criticized the crime scene investigation techniques, the legal strategies, and the script dialogue.

"Why do you watch this show, Sal? You hate everything about it."

"I love it. It's like a game. I keep score, and every time that da-dum noise hits, it's like the end of a round." One day he crunched on a biscuit and looked over at Juno. "You know what that sound really is? It's the door at Riker's Island when it shuts behind you. Da-dum. Sounds like never. That's what the door says at Riker's. When am I getting out? Not ever. Never."

"You went to Riker's?"

"Mmhmm. Once or twice. That was the early years. Look at him eating a doughnut over the body. No cop does that. Ridiculous."

"Maybe we should watch *Wheel of Fortune*."

"Shut your mouth, girlie. God forbid. Put me in the old folks' home with those poor Jell-O-eating rascals."

Juno liked to imagine how her grandmother would have gotten along with Sal. She hated *Wheel of Fortune*, too. She really couldn't stand the "Before and After" category. She turn livid. "It's a Wonderful Life Jacket! What in hell is that supposed to mean?" *Yes*, Juno, thought, *they'd have hit it off*.

Sal told Juno all about what happened with Monk's father. How Monk had come to Brattleboro with his mother in the middle of the night. "From the moment Ray was gone, Gloria only cared about one thing. Monk. She'd always called him Monk, you know. After some book she read. Gloria and her books. Anyway, she didn't sit around crying and hanging onto her rosary. She packed a bag and left Nutley. Didn't tell a soul. Back then you didn't have to go far to disappear."

"You came with her?"

"Not exactly. Not at first. Lookit the guy's walking —he just went right through your crime scene, you big dummy. That's an acquittal, right there."

His eyes watered at the edges and he reached into his sleeve for a tissue. "Are you tired, Sal? I can come back tomorrow."

"Don't you talk to me like that, madam. I'm not that old. The mileage is all highway."

"I think you've got that backward, Sal."

"Says you. Listen. Monk, he's not like us. Even when he was a kid. He wasn't meant for the rough stuff."

"You think I'm meant for the rough stuff, Sal?"

Sal sat back and pretended to consider her for the first time. "Girlie, I think you are meant for the win. And I think you are built to survive. I'd bet on it."

THIRTY-TWO

"You're right, lady. This is a lot more interesting than today's *Law & Order*. They got the damn SUV marathon anyway. I can't watch that. Who watches that? But I love that Jerry Orbach. Listen, one night, when he was in *Guys and Dolls*..."

"Sal, nothing would make me happier than to hear this Jerry Orbach story, but in person."

"Yeah, get the hell out of that house. Are you sure this is all you need from me? This is, what, two, three phone calls. What else can I do?"

"Nothing, Sal. You're my hero already. Get my coffee ready and I'll be there soon."

"One word from you, girlie. One word."

"I know, Sal. Thank you."

"Hey, wait. You want me to call Monk?"

Juno was about to say no, but she changed her mind. "Yes, Sal. But give me a few minutes. Call him and make sure I got through. Just in case something happens and I can't get to him."

By the time Sal called and Monk answered, everything was coming together. Monk didn't ask for details and Sal didn't offer them. "She's safe, Sal?" That was his only question.

"She will be. Your girl is smart. She's a captain. A CEO. And not bad looking."

"She's too smart for me, Sal."

"No, no. Better keep this one, Monk. One day she's gonna have your back."

"I'm staying on the wall, Sally. No need for anybody to look after me."

"I'm not going to live forever, Monk. You know what that will mean."

"Nobody's coming, Sal. It's been almost twenty years."

"No, it hasn't. They came. You know that."

"I know, Sal. It's over. They're all gone."

"Not all of them. They'll never all be gone."

Juno didn't hear anything of that particular conversation between Monk and Sal. But Sal had told her that there were people out there watching Monk, that he wasn't as well-hidden as he thought. He was, Sal told her, well-protected. He had followed Gloria and the boy to Brattleboro after his brother Ray's death in order to see that they were safe. He had made promises to ensure their safety. He'd had to do some favors and make some promises. But his brother's family—his family—was safe.

"Didn't you ever want to get married, Sal?"

"Why, darling, this is so unexpected," Sal whispered, laying a hand on his heart. Juno gave him a little shove. "No, I didn't. One time I did, but she..."

Juno watched Sal's eyes brighten. "She was married already."

"She was. Very happily. I could never have taken her from a happy home. Her happiness was more beautiful to me than my own." Sal spoke slowly, as if thinking it out. "I have no regrets," he finished. "Do you believe in the saints?"

"I didn't get much religion growing up, Sal. I like your statues in the yard. I especially like that one in the corner by all the bird feeders."

"Come, come." Sal had beckoned her to the hall closet, where he pulled out a shoe box with smaller boxes and velvet bags inside. "That's St. Teresa of Avila. She's good for you. Take this," he said, handing Juno a small pouch. Inside, Juno found a coin-sized oval with the figure of a woman. On one side, it said, "Fear Nothing," and on the other it read, "All Things Are Passing Things."

Juno summoned herself back to the present, reaching into the small pocket of her jeans, where she had placed the St. Teresa medal. She felt the ridges on its face. *Fear nothing*, she said to herself. She reached into the safe and took the last two burner phones, then walked back to the main house.

THIRTY-THREE

She didn't know how Mitchell got out of Turkey, but she could find no trace of him when she had returned to the house. Her passport was still in the nightstand drawer—she'd half expected it to be gone and had made a plan. But once she'd gotten into the taxi with the ragged suitcase and her small sack of actual belongings, she'd begun to feel the electricity of winning again. At the counter, the crunch of the stamp on her passport and boarding pass sounded like music. She waited in the regular security check line for the first time in years, making faces at the toddler peeking over his father's shoulder in front of her.

A ticket had been waiting for her at the Lufthansa counter. One of the maids had found an old suitcase for her to use; it wasn't that she had anything at all to carry, but flying without luggage attracts a tremendous amount of unwanted attention. She wasn't running, she reminded herself. She was backing away, the way you did when you met a bear or a snake in your path. As long as she kept moving, it would be over soon.

She hoped it would be over. She couldn't yet imagine what would seem like a real escape from Mitchell. Could she feel safe with him in jail? She tried not to wish him dead; she tried very hard. She tried to think back to any intimacy with him that could help her see him as another human being, but it took more energy than she could spend on him right now. Right now, she knew he would keep coming for her until something prevented him from coming. And he wouldn't be trying to protect himself now that she had revealed his secrets. He'd be coming for revenge.

That was, if he knew it was her. As she handed over the suitcase that held a couple of blankets from the market and little else, she brightened a little. The police wouldn't likely explain the source of the information. It was verifiable enough without tracking the source. And Mitchell wouldn't think her capable. His under-estimation of her—he would fold with the winning hand because he'd never see her bluff. She might just walk away.

For most of the way, she forgot to be afraid. At the folding tables, she took off her running-away shoes one more time and placed them in the bucket. *Let's be lucky one more time*, she thought, looking at how ragged the laces had become. She laid her bag in the next bucket, heaving them both onto the conveyor belt. In her sock feet with nothing to do with her hands, she stood waiting to walk through the security arch.

No beep, no red light. She sighed in relief and went to get her things. She waited. The man and the toddler who had been ahead of her were putting on their shoes, the little boy running and laughing. She waved as they walked away toward the gates.

The girls behind her finished putting on her jacket and sneakers. The next couple moved some things from a small piece of luggage to their carry-on bags, sliding back into their canvas loafers. She looked back into the scanning tunnel. Where were her things?

This is it, she thought. She was caught. By the police, by Mitchell's men, by somebody. She wheeled around until she saw her bag and shoes on the inspection table over behind the scanner. Two men in gray caps stood over her things, one replacing the items in her bag while the other put her shoes on his hands, marching them across the table.

She never knew their names. But they smiled when they saw her, and the one with her shoes on his hands waved, her shoe dancing back and forth over his head. Then he brought her things to her so she wouldn't have to cross back into the line. "Very sorry," he said, smiling. "You are leaving Turkey alone?"

"Yes." She gulped, still waiting.

"Very sorry," he said, smiling again. "We will see you again one day, we hope. You are all good. You can go home now. You can go anywhere!" He made motions with his hands as he had when he marched her shoes around the table.

"Yes," she said, resisting the urge to hug him. "Thank you so very much. I'm going home now."

Home, Juno thought. The word hadn't meant this much to her in a very long time.

THIRTY-FOUR

She stared out the window all the way to Frankfurt. Watching the miles, the changing landscape below, made the remaining menace dissolve. *All things are passing things.* A door in her life closed slowly, and she took one last look at what almost happened to her before she let all the pieces fall down through the clouds, scattered them across Eastern Europe so that terrible vision would never be real again.

She checked into an hourly pod hotel in Terminal 1 to wait for her connecting flight. Something about the efficiency of the tiny room, its loft bed with storage and the plastic partition hiding a full shower and toilet, satisfied her immensely. She found herself wishing she could stay for days in this bright white chamber, as if it was a psychological decompression tank. The door had a tinted porthole so she could see people passing in the hall, but no one could see in. She climbed the ladder in a giddy mood, happy to be alone in her own private bed, oddly not even thinking of Monk for the first time in weeks and weeks. The small television built into the ceiling above the bed had a few channels in English, but she found a *Law & Order* marathon on a German channel. Juno snuggled down and pulled the fluffy white comforter over her eyes, letting herself fall asleep to the rhythmic da-dum sound of a door closing behind her. This time, she was on the right side of it. She began to believe she could be free.

The pod alarm went off fifteen minutes before her checkout time, two hours before her flight to Kennedy. Juno turned over and saw a man standing at the porthole window. She only saw the back of his head, but he had an earpiece and seemed to be talking to someone. She gathered the sheet around herself and eased slowly down the ladder. She knew he couldn't see her, but she ducked beneath the window and tried to listen. She felt her cheeks turning red; she wasn't sure if it was panic or anger or both. She could only hear a little, and the man was speaking German. Numbers, she thought. Or times.

She dressed quickly. She considered calling someone—Monk, or Sal—and for a brief moment she felt a wave of gratitude that there were in fact people she could call. But as she looked up, the man was gone from the window. She stared at the phone, then put it back in her bag. What could they do, anyway, from so far away? She remembered Sal taking the medal out of its velvet sack and placing it on her palm.

"She was a brave girl, headstrong. She ran away with her brother."

"That's my people, right there," Juno had said to him.

"She wanted to become a martyr. She convinced her brother they should go find some infidels and get beheaded."

"That's a little much, even for the trailer park I crawled out of." Juno touched the folds in the woman's robe where they stood in ridges on the medal. "I had a brother," she began. "And I talked him into running away."

"It's okay," Sal said. "St. Teresa and her brother got caught, too."

"Oh, we didn't get caught." Juno shook her head. "Nobody looked for us."

Sal patted her cheek. "You get lost in this world again, I will come and find you." Juno's eyes watered. "She liked romance novels," Sal added.

"Wait. What?" Juno looked at Sal and laughed. "You're kidding me."

"Not at all. Her mother loved romance novels, and Teresa helped her hide them from her father, who was brutal and strict."

"Well, Sal. Maybe I've got some saint in me after all. All I've known up to now was the sinner."

Fear nothing. In her new life, Juno held the cards. She picked up her bag, opened the door, and walked out into the hallway. The empty hallway. She looked both ways at the row of doors with portholes and saw no one.

She turned the corner toward the entrance and there he was, the man with the earpiece. He was behind the front desk, arranging a tray of room key cards. When he saw Juno, he beamed.

"Guten Tag," he said, with a little bow. "Thank you for staying with us. Have a safe trip!"

THIRTY-FIVE

The flight landed at Kennedy around six p.m.. Juno had a free row for most of the flight but ended up talking to two young German women in the row across the aisle for the last few hours. They were going on a cross-country tour of the United States, beginning in New York and zigzagging through the Appalachian Mountains, New Orleans, Texas, up through the Southwest, and on to Seattle, where they were meeting a friend who was studying abroad at the University of Washington. Juno found herself offering everything from restaurant and hotel suggestions to driving directions.

"Once you get out of North Carolina, I-40 is a great ride. Knoxville, Nashville, Memphis, the Mississippi Delta—that's the cradle of American civilization. Do you like music? Country? Blues?"

"We love blues! We want to go to the crossroads and meet the demon who taught Robert Johnson."

"Well, first of all, it was not just any demon, it was the Devil. And that place they call the crossroads isn't the real one. But you'll figure it out. Hey, when you get to Memphis, go to Beale Street. Don't listen to any of those barkers, the men on the street trying to call you into their restaurants. Go to Miss Polly's and get the apple pie." She felt the strongest urge to take Monk there, immediately. She wanted him to sit at the counter with her and taste the closest thing to her grandmother's pie. She wanted to take him to Red's in Clarksdale. She wanted to walk through the Marigny in New Orleans holding his hand. That was her family. Her life might not have many people. But it had places. Places that had made her. She had never wanted to share that with anyone.

For some reason, the girls were very excited to see Area 51. "I mean, it's cute. A little silly."

"No alien autopsy?"

"Trust me. No. Do not follow any man in a van who promises he can show you one, either."

"And we have to see Las Vegas! Viva Las Vegas! We want to win big money and see the dancers. We want to see Celine Dion!"

It took a good five minutes for Juno to stop laughing. She tried to explain it to the girls, but the language barrier made it a little difficult for them to get the full picture.

"Well, ladies. I guess the short version is this: I met the love of my life in Las Vegas, Nevada."

"Ahhh!" the girls said together, giggling. "Did you go to a chapel? Did Elvis marry you?"

Juno scrunched up her face. "No, we didn't. But hey, there's a reason to go back now. I tell you, though, there is the one show you have got to see. The story is kind of sad, but you won't believe the way they dance on this wall that comes up..."

Juno told them every detail she could remember, waving her hands around and humming the music. People in the seats in front and back of her leaned in to listen to the story.

THIRTY-SIX

Juno stretched and helped the German girls get their backpacks out of the overhead compartments while they waited for the first-class cabin to empty. They hugged her like sisters when they said goodbye at the end of the jetway. Juno didn't bother to pick up the ragged suitcase full of blankets that day. Nor did she pick it up when the airline emailed her about finding her lost bag. She hoped somebody was keeping warm with them and admiring their light texture. She needed no souvenirs of that trip. *We will see you again one day*. She'd go to the Hagia Sophia one day. For better reasons. Her own reasons.

Washing up, she looked at herself in the mirror. She read someplace about a guy who would see himself in the mirror every morning and say, "Hey, buddy. Let's see what we can do." She decided to give it a try. "Hey, bud—"

She couldn't finish. The tears flooded out. In the

mirror, she had seen Jack's eyes instead of her own. The look of care and genuine concern. She had given the look to herself, the look she hadn't seen since he left. She let it out, sobs echoing off the tile walls. She washed her face again with cool water, blotting it dry with a handful of paper towels. Finally, a little girl, maybe eight years old, came out of the last stall.

"I'm afraid to fly, too," she said. "But it's okay because my brother is going with me. Do you have someone going with you?"

"Yes." Juno nodded hard. "I have somebody." The girl smiled and turned to go. "Wait," Juno said, fishing into her pocket. "Take this. She's already helped me." The girl paused, then held out her hand. Juno dropped the St. Teresa medal into it, and the girl darted away.

Walking down the concourse, Juno felt the hollowed spot in her left shoe wearing away just as she passed the Burberry store. Minutes later, she walked out in a pair of chunky black boots and a new trench coat. She was glad she'd kept that cash from the game in the lining of her bag.

New shoes always made her feel more confident. Whether they were her annual new pair of white Keds growing up or a fancy pair of Burberry boots. She'd catch a cab into the city and stay in her favorite hotel down on the Lower East Side, maybe take a sunset walk. Maybe just sit on the rooftop terrace. Tomorrow, she'd decide what to do. Right now, she needed to feel like the old Juno again so that she could face whatever might be waiting.

She wondered what they thought had happened. Did Sal tell them she called? Would Monk understand why it was Sal she turned to when she needed help, the kind of help Sal would know how to provide? Monk turned away from that life. He'd had the opportunity to move past it. Juno had spent most of her life choosing from a set of mostly bad options. The way she saw it, she had to be alive, and free, to make it back to Monk. They couldn't run and hide forever. No matter how much fun they knew how to have. She'd brought the danger to his door, to his mother's door. Sal had spent his life keeping Monk and his family out of danger. No matter what happened, she knew she'd made the right decision.

Monk. Surely he knew she wouldn't have run away unless she'd had no choice. Had he looked for her? Sal didn't say. But she hadn't asked. Had Monk dreamed about her as she dreamed about him? Had he walked to the river of the missing people? Did he ask them if they had seen her? Was that how she found her way to his window from halfway around the world?

Tomorrow she would wake up. She would be the real Juno again, feet on the ground and head on straight. She'd decide whether to take the train or rent a car. She'd go to Brattleboro and surprise them all. And they'd be happy to see her. She smiled when she thought that maybe tomorrow night she'd be eating potato soup and drinking a nice Belgian ale playing backgammon with Mr. Thompson. In the two-way security mirror, she saw herself smiling. It was real. Yes, she'd rent a car and go by the bakery to get Gloria's cake. She walked a little faster, because she had some-place to go.

She was coming around the corner, leaving the concourse and the security area. That's when she saw him. She thought she was imagining things. But he was also very, very real.

Monk. He almost dropped the flowers when he saw her. Tears clouding her vision, she dropped her bag and ran to him. He caught her, hugging her so long and hard her feet left the ground. "I'm not letting you go ever, ever, ever again," he whispered. Or did she say those words herself?

He kissed her, and she felt the electricity of a winning hand, times ten.

"Where do you want to go?"

"Home," she said. "Let's go home."

———

"Well, you keep eyes on him. Like I said. No, I hear you. Better them than us, that's what I say. If the Feds can't find him, he's gonna stay right there. No, I told you, I promised her. She just has to say the word. Yeah, well, I'm with you on that one. No, it's good news. Hey, it's great news for us. Let me know if anything changes. All right, then. Say hello to Irene. Kiss the kids. Next week, right."

Sal hung up the phone. Monk texted him that he

had found Juno at the airport. Sal texted him back a thumbs-up.

He'd known a lot of terrible men. He had lived in the places terrible men go. His mother once told him, "Nobody comes to this house thinking it's the Vatican. If they come here, it's not absolution they're trying to find."

Sal grew up understanding retribution. He learned how to make the guilty pay. It was the gift he had to offer, and he had no others that he knew of. And this guy, this Mitchell guy, XKC3PO whatever he was. He was guilty of a lot.

———

Juno waited. She had three of a kind, sevens. It was a good hand. She was waiting for the river card. She didn't know what it would be this time.

The online poker tournaments weren't nearly as fun for her, and she couldn't read the room as well at first. But she found after a few months that she picked up different things, habits. People still had tells; they just weren't as obvious. But there weren't a lot of poker games on Paros. What there was on Paros: cats, scooters, goats, the most amazing seafood, swimming every day in the blue Aegean sea. There was even a Byzantine church. Not the Hagia Sophia, but a beautiful place that dated back centuries. Juno had walked almost the whole island and she never got tired of finding new views.

Monk did all of his work remotely, too. It wasn't much of a change from his globetrotting lifestyle before. In fact, he'd adopted much more regular hours. Once in a while, Pilot Alan would take them off for a weekend in Paris or Florence. They'd even gone to Norway once when Juno wanted to see snow. Gloria came and stayed for a month; by the time she left, she'd learned enough Greek to talk to their neighbors. They'd be back in Brattleboro for Christmas, of course, they told her. For now, it was safe here, surrounded by the blue that floated Odysseus.

Mitchell had disappeared. Another lost person. The FBI had tried to arrest him at his New York apartment where he'd last been seen, but they missed him somehow, and the trail had gone cold. Sal couldn't even find him. At least that's what he said. It should have been enough. That was something else Sal said. But for Juno, it wasn't enough. She knew as long as Mitchell was drawing breath, he'd come for her one day. And for anybody who got in his way.

She thought about that last card game with Sal. Not even poker; it wasn't Tuesday, so they didn't have the boys to play. It was just Juno and Sal. He was still teaching her pinochle and marveling that there was still a card game out there she hadn't learned.

"I don't know how to play Bridge, either." Juno shook her head, picking cashews out of Sal's bowl of nuts.

"You're messing up my proportions. Now I've got to go get some more cashews." Sal padded off to his kitchen. Juno studied the sparkles in the Formica table on Sal's patio, the same mint ice cream green as her grandma's kitchen table. "You want a Limoncello?"

"Mmm hmm." Juno chewed and thought. "Hey, Sal?"

Sal came back with a bowl and two small glasses. "Yes, darling?" He smiled, his eyes wrinkling up. "What is not perfect in your world?"

"Well, Sal," she started, then stopped to think it through. "Do you remember the first time I met you? You were telling the fellas about a warehouse. One that was going to be demolished, and what somebody might find when it went down."

Sal set the glasses and bowl down so he could take Juno's hands. She had tears in her eyes. "I won't lie to you, girlie."

She looked at him. "I don't need to know where. Just, is there maybe a new warehouse going up? With a solid foundation?"

"We don't know where he is. I swear to you. And I will swear this: I will keep you safe. On my life. On Monk's life. And you know he is like a son to me. Both of you will be safe."

She had whispered one more time, her voice shaking, her eyes pleading. "Sal, I won't tell anyone. You know I won't. Please tell me he's gone."

But Sal had only kissed her hand and then put the glass in it. Juno knew. Sal didn't have Mitchell. Mitchell was out there. One day, he'd be around a corner.

It took her less than a week to convince Monk to move to Greece. They moved to a small fishing village, a white house in the cliffs with a beautiful view and enough of a WiFi signal for both of them to work. The locals called them William and Tamara. The kept to themselves. They called Sal once a week on a phone they kept in a post office box in town.

Juno finished the round up for the day, and then she left the game. She closed the laptop and tucked it into its sleeve. Monk crossed the patio and embraced her from behind, kissing her neck until she giggled, suddenly ticklish as a little girl.

"You know, when I first saw you, I had no idea your hair was a wig. It's funny—"

"That was a great wig," Juno said, tossing her very real long, blond hair. Monk had cut his shaggy locks crisp and short on the sides, but he left it longer on top. Juno loved the scratchy sides of his head, and she grazed her cheek against him.

"Well, I like you both ways."

"Oh, you like me?" Juno slid the edge of her kimono off of her shoulder, golden from months on the island.

"A little," Monk said as she let the robe fall, revealing her bare body. She'd taken her swimsuit off in the hopes he'd come find her. Juno slid her hand along his waist until she reached the buttons in the front of his shorts. She reached down between his legs to feel him growing hard at the sight of her. Her hands freed the button of his shorts as they fell to the ground; she felt his breath draw in.

Monk pulled her hips forward and set her on top of the patio bar, planting his lips just above her navel. Juno felt so free, naked on the most beautiful island, with the warm sun and smell of the sea filling the air. He moved his tongue down lower while he spread her legs apart. Gently his lips and tongue moved up and down, penetrating her softly. She threw her head back, moaning as she let herself completely go. She pulled his head up to steady herself as his mouth found her breasts, playfully flicking each nipple until she let out a shriek of delight. He knew she loved that.

Monk pulled his head back, grabbed her off the bar, and carried her to the blanket on the grass she laid out earlier. It was her favorite place to sit and look at the sea. He kissed her deeply while softly touching her everywhere. He moved his hands between her legs again, spreading them gently. His fingers lightly massaged her clit until she began to moan and squirm beneath his touch. Until he slid his finger deep inside, making her scream out in ecstasy. He moved his finger in and out slowly until she couldn't take it anymore. She pushed him to the side and climbed on top as she eased herself down onto his lap. She could feel him hard beneath her as she rocked on top of him. He moaned, "Fuck! You feel so good..."

Monk slid his hands down her sides of her hips, pushing her harder into his erection. As his hands moved behind her, inside her thighs, she shrieked again.

Juno stopped and rolled him on top of her while covering his mouth with a deep, deep kiss. His hands settled in her hair as he kissed her deeply. She loved the way he felt against her skin. She tilted her hips as he put himself inside her immediately, deep and stiff, and her body closed around him. He pulled all the way back and paused before slowly entering her again, his hips slightly swaying and bucking with pleasure. He thrust even deeper; she lifted her hips and squirmed against him. Monk began to moan softly whispering her name in pleasure. "Juno…"

The movement of his hips and the penetration sent her; "Oh my God!" She grabbed onto his ass with both hands, pulling him deeper. She hung onto him as the orgasm continued in waves. Monk joined in, moaning loudly, his body stiffening as he came inside her. They collapsed, in each other's arms, relaxing and listening to the sound of the waves.

He pulled her close and kissed her, his lips, soft, salty-sweet.

————

The mornings were beautiful. Juno felt like she was finally beginning to relax a little at least. Her days were spent swimming, playing poker, making love, and eating Monk's delicious food. He seemed to be taking to the island life quite nicely.

She felt safe with Monk. A foreign feeling she was afraid to get used to. She walked into the kitchen, and Monk kissed her on each cheek and her head. "Have a good swim. I'll get some breakfast going."

Juno turned to head out toward the patio, leaving Monk alone in the kitchen with his cooking devices. Walking through the patio the stones felt warm under her bare feet. She walked through the garden and the grass down to the steppingstones that made a pathway down to the beach. The beach was warm, but the water was cold on her feet. She shivered and sank, pushing herself out for her morning swim.

Monk stepped out and watched Juno from the patio. As he saw her gliding out toward the yachts anchored just offshore, he went back into the house. He pulled a blue wooden chair away from its place at the table and over to the kitchen sink. He stood on the chair to reach a decorative ceramic pitcher on the top shelf. It had been there since they'd moved in. Once he had it, he pulled it down and set it on the counter. When he stepped off the chair, he reached inside and pulled out a phone.

"Sal. No, she's swimming. Yes. I am a lucky man. But I'd like you to make me a happy man and tell me you found him."

Before You Go...

If you enjoyed my book please take a quick second to leave a short review on Amazon. These reviews help me as an author be found by other amazing readers like you.

Thank you so much! :)

About the Author

Shilo West is the author of the High Stakes series. She loves to write mafia/billionaire adventure type romances. Lucky enough to live in Maui with her dog and fiancée, when she's not writing, she loves hanging out at the beach or hiking.

Keep up with the latest updates & sneak peeks here:
https://www.cravepublishing.net/shilo-west